Home Where the Heart Is

Home to Collingsworth
Book 1

by

Kimberly Rae Jordan

THREE**STRAND**
P R E S S

A CORD OF THREE STRANDS IS NOT EASILY BROKEN.

A man, a woman & their God.
Three Strand Press publishes Christian Romance stories
that intertwine love, faith and family.
Always clean. Always heartwarming. Always uplifting.

❧ Chapter One ❧

VIOLET flipped on her blinker to exit the highway and begin the final leg of her journey. A sense of reluctance pressed down on her with increasing weight as each mile passed beneath her car. Three days ago a phone call had started this trip, and now it was almost over. She sure wished she could turn the car around and go in any direction but the one she was headed in.

Patches of snow still lay beneath the trees lining the winding road that rose and fell with the gentle hills of northeastern Minnesota. Late March in Seattle meant spring was well underway, but here in the Midwest it wasn't unusual to still see some snow on the ground. Snowstorms were even a possibility. Thankfully, there was nothing of that sort forecasted for the next few days. A funeral was bad enough, but having to bury someone on a cold, gray day was so much worse.

The sign saying it was just two more miles to her destination loomed before her. Violet gripped the wheel and let out a long breath. She'd had plenty of time to think over the past three days, but there had been no great revelations on how she should handle everything that was sure to transpire over the next week. The last time they'd all been together had been just after her graduation. Tension had been high as Gran had made it known exactly how she felt about Violet's plans to venture out on her own. But that eighteen year old girl was not to be swayed.

The quick wail of a siren brought her thoughts back to the road. She looked into the rear view mirror to see flashing lights behind her. Gritting her teeth, Violet guided the car to a stop on the shoulder of the road and put it in park. In her side mirror, she saw the door of the patrol car open and a man get out. He put a hat on his head and began to walk in her direction, his strides long and sure.

Violet rolled down her window as he reached the car door. She glanced at the man's uniform, lifting a brow at the sheriff's badge pinned to the jacket he wore. "Wow, the town must be short on officers if the sheriff is out pulling people over."

"It's my duty to serve as needed," the man said as he braced a hand on the roof of her car. "May I see your license and registration, please?"

Violet reached for her purse and fished out her license and the car's registration. "What did I do wrong?" she asked as she handed them to him. As their gazes met, Violet found herself looking into the bluest set of eyes she'd ever seen.

"You were speeding," he said, glancing up as a car passed by them on the road heading out of town.

"Was I?" Violet glanced at her dashboard. "Guess the speedometer really is busted."

The man cleared his throat. "Your speedometer is broken?"

Violet bit her lip. Maybe that was a bit of information she should have kept to herself. "Well, it must be if you're saying I was speeding, because I didn't think I was."

The man held her gaze for a moment before looking back down at her documents. Violet watched him, taking in his firm jaw and the little bit of short brown hair that showed beneath his hat. She didn't recognize him, but then it had been a few years since she'd last been in town.

His brow furrowed as he looked up from her license. "Collingsworth?"

Violet sighed. "Yep. I'm one of those."

"You've come home for Miss Julia's funeral," the man stated.

"Yes."

"You're Jessa's sister?" he asked.

"One of them," Violet answered with a nod.

"Well, I'll let you off with a warning this time." He handed the documents back to her. "But get that speedometer checked."

"Nice to know the Collingsworth name still holds some clout around here," Violet remarked drily. "I think I'd almost rather have the ticket."

The man tilted his head to the side. "That could be arranged."

Violet held up her hands. "No, no. I'm sorry. There's a reason I left this town years ago, and I'm afraid it's all coming back now."

"Well, my condolences on the loss of your grandmother."

Violet reined in her emotions and responded as Gran would have expected her to. With a nod of her head, she said, "Thank you."

As the sheriff turned to walk away, Violet asked him, "What's your name?"

"Dean Marconett."

"Well, Sheriff Dean Marconett, it's a pleasure to meet you." Violet stuck her hand out the window.

The sheriff's grip was firm as he shook her hand. "The pleasure is mine."

Violet watched in her mirror as he walked back to his car. She clasped her hands together, still feeling the warmth of his hand as it had held hers. He didn't pull out right away, so she figured he was waiting on her. Staring straight ahead, she put her car in gear and pulled back out onto the road. A glance in her mirror a little ways down the road revealed that the sheriff was following her.

He didn't have to worry about her speeding now. Violet was in no hurry to arrive in Collingsworth, the town founded by her family many, many years ago.

Welcome to Collingsworth! Population: 11, 645

She passed the sign with a sense of going beyond the point of no return. Unfortunately, she couldn't just not show up. During her call to Jessa the night before, Violet had let her know she'd be arriving today. The road turned into Main Street, and as she drove, Violet saw that although much had changed, there were still a lot of familiar places like *Ben's Diner* and *Lucy's Clip & Style*. She imagined it was no longer Lucy doing hair since the woman had already been quite old when Violet had left a decade earlier.

She looked in her mirror again and saw that the sheriff's car was no longer behind her. Violet slowly drove the length of Main Street and exited the town to the northeast. It didn't take long to reach the turnoff to the long driveway that led to her childhood home. Collingsworth Manor.

With her heart pounding, Violet guided her car along the tree-lined driveway until that final turn when the manor came into view. She passed through the open gates, over the small cement bridge and eased on the brakes, coming to a stop just shy of the steps to the front door. Closing her eyes, Violet said a brief prayer for guidance and then opened the door and got out. Her body wasn't used to so much inactivity and felt stiff as she stretched her arms to the sky. Despite what lay ahead, the beauty of the manor's surroundings brought her a measure of peace. She loved nature and this was the place where that love had sprung to life.

"Vi!" An excited shout drew her attention.

Turning, she saw one of her younger sisters come flying down the steps of the manor toward her. Violet opened her arms to embrace Lily. This was the only thing she'd looked forward to on this trip.

"Hey, sweetness! How are you?" Violet held her at arm's length and took in how much her sister had grown and matured. At seventeen she'd blossomed into a beautiful young woman. Unfortunately, Violet had witnessed most of that growth over online chats. "You look amazing."

"You too, Vi! I love your hair," the younger girl gushed. "I told you to let it grow."

The youngest Collingsworth followed more slowly. At ten years old, Rose had only been a few months old when Violet had left the manor and Collingsworth. It had been a rough year leading up to her birth, and Violet had desperately needed to escape. "Hi, Rosie belle."

The young girl gave her a shy smile, but allowed Violet to draw her into a hug.

With an arm around each of their shoulders, Violet walked with them to the front door of the manor. She couldn't help but notice some of the disrepair of the house. It didn't seem to fit with how her grandmother had always cared for the building that had been in her family since the start of the town.

"Jessa!" Lily called as they entered the house. "Violet's here!"

It took a minute, but soon their eldest sister appeared in the doorway leading to the kitchen. She carried a vase of bright flowers in her hands. She set them on the table near the door and then held out her arms to Violet. As she embraced her sister, Violet felt a rush of love. Though they were part of the most difficult years of her life, her sisters were still her only family.

"You made decent time," Jessa said. "I thought maybe you wouldn't get here until supper."

Violet shrugged sheepishly. "I might have been speeding part of the way."

Jessa raised a brow and gave her a stern look. "Did you get a ticket?"

"Well, apparently it still pays to be a Collingsworth. The sheriff let me off with a warning."

"Dean pulled you over?"

"Yep. By the way, do you have a reputable mechanic? I guess I'd better get my speedometer looked at."

Jessa laughed and shook her head, exasperation clear on her face. "Welcome home, dear sister!"

Violet smiled and felt some of the tension ease from her. Maybe this wouldn't be as bad as she had thought it would be. Already the lack of her grandmother's oppressive presence was making a difference in how she viewed this place.

"When are the others supposed to be here?" Violet asked as she went with Jessa into the kitchen, the younger girls following behind them.

"Laurel is arriving later today, I think," Jessa said as she opened the fridge and pulled out a pitcher of juice.

"And Cami?"

Jessa shut the fridge door with a little more force than necessary. "Who knows."

"Have you spoken to her?" Violet had left a few messages, but hadn't been able to reach her directly.

"Nope. I stopped trying after leaving five voice mails." Jessa took down some glasses from the cupboard and slapped it shut. "She knows when the funeral is. It's up to her whether she shows or not."

Tension began to creep back up her neck. Jessa and Cami had always conflicted, and Violet had always been caught in the middle. It looked like this gathering would be no different.

She rubbed her forehead. "I'll try her again a little later."

"Let's have some cookies and juice," Jessa suggested with a smile, albeit a tight one. "Rose and Lily made them this morning."

"I'm sure they're wonderful," Violet said as she took the

glass of juice from Jessa. She bit into a cookie and smiled. "Yes, I was right. They are delicious."

Somehow they had to make it through this next week without killing each other, and then they could get on with their separate lives. The thought brought a mixture of relief and sadness.

After they finished their snack, Violet stood. "You girls want to help me unload my car?" She glanced at Jessa. "Same room?"

"Yep. It's all ready for you."

Violet rounded the counter and hugged Jessa. "I'm glad to see you again. And I'm sorry about Gran. You were close to her, so I know this loss is hardest for you."

Jessa's arms tightened around her. Violet held her older sister as she cried, realizing with all the responsibility that had fallen on her with their grandmother's death, she probably hadn't had much time to grieve. If Violet could help her with that now, she was glad to do it. Jessa being Jessa, she didn't let her emotions rule her long. She stepped back and swiped at the wetness on her cheeks.

"Let's get you unpacked and settled," she said in her no-nonsense tone.

Outside, the girls looked at the stuff in the car with wide eyes.

"Are you coming home for good?" Lily asked. Violet didn't miss the hopeful glance she sent her way.

"No, but I was in the process of moving when Jessa called about Gran, so I just loaded all my stuff up and came."

"So you're homeless?"

Violet smiled at Rose's question. "Well, technically you could say that, but I had some leads on another place to say, so I wouldn't have been homeless. My roommate is moving out of her apartment at the end of this month. Rather than leave my stuff and pay for storage while I came here, I just decided to bring it with me."

"And this is all your stuff? No beds or anything?" Rose

opened the back door of the car.

"Nope. I always rented furnished places. Just easier to not have all that stuff tying me down since I tend to move a lot."

"Do you want us to bring it all in?" Lily asked.

"For right now, we'll bring in the things I'll need for the next few days. I packed so I could just take out those bags."

Violet leaned into the car and pulled out the bags she would need. As she set them on the ground, she heard an engine and the crunch of tires on the pavement of the driveway. She turned toward where the driveway curved, hoping it would be Cami or Laurel.

❧ *Chapter Two* ❧

DEAN wasn't altogether sure why he had made his way out to Collingsworth Manor. He told himself it was because he wanted to give Violet Collingsworth the name of a reliable mechanic and to offer his condolences to the sisters. It certainly wasn't because the brown-eyed woman he'd stopped for speeding had piqued his curiosity.

Over the years he'd wondered about Violet Collingsworth and her other absent sisters. To meet her in person, completely by chance, had just increased his interest in the young woman Julia Collingsworth had told him not to help...should she ever come to him with certain questions.

As he rounded the last turn of the long winding driveway, Dean spotted three of the sisters standing next to the older model car. He pulled to a stop behind it and picked up his hat from the seat next to him. He put it on out of habit as he stepped from the car.

"Sheriff Marconett," Violet said as he approached them. "I can almost guarantee I wasn't speeding this time." She gave him a wide grin, a sparkle in her chocolate brown eyes.

"How do you know for sure? Your speedometer being

broken and all," Dean responded, working to keep a serious expression on his face.

She laughed then, a husky sound that warmed him. "Well, you do have a point."

"Dean!" He looked past Violet to see Jessa coming toward them. "I thought maybe the car I heard was Laurel or Cami."

Dean smiled ruefully. "Sorry to disappoint, Jessa."

He saw a similarity to Violet in the smile Jessa gave him. He knew they only shared a mother, which could account for the resemblance in feature but difference in coloring. Jessa's fiery red hair, pale skin and tall, slender stature were in direct contrast to the nearly black hair and olive skin of her sister. Violet was also shorter by a couple of inches and had a completely different build than Jessa. But in their eyes and smiles, he could see their likeness.

"No disappointment," Jessa assured him with a warm smile. "What brings the sheriff out our way?"

He gestured to Violet's car. "I thought I'd come by and give your sister the name of a mechanic who could help her out with her speedometer problem."

"Ah, she did ask me if I knew of someone." Jessa glanced at Violet. "I'll make sure she gets it taken care of right away."

"*I'll* make sure it gets taken care of," Violet said, wrinkling her nose at Jessa. "I've been taking care of myself for a while now."

"And yet you drove halfway across the country in a car with a broken speedometer," Jessa pointed out with a frown.

Dean held his breath, hoping he hadn't sparked a disagreement between them. He didn't know Violet at all, but he knew Jessa could be wound pretty tight sometimes. She took after her grandmother in that.

But no negative emotion crossed Violet's face. Instead she just smiled and said, "Okay. You've got a point. But in my defense, I didn't have time to get anything done to it before leaving."

Dean was surprised to see Jessa's expression relax. "You

know I just worry about you."

Violet slipped an arm around her sister's waist. "I know you do. It will get taken care of right away. Promise."

She reached into the pocket of her faded jeans and pulled out her phone. "Okay, someone give me the info, and I'll give them a call today."

Dean took out his own cell and found the name and number in his contact list. He handed her the phone, noticing as she took it that her nails were neatly trimmed but completely unpolished.

"I've copied the information and will call as soon as I've got my stuff unloaded. And I'm going to use both your names. Surely one of you will put the fear of God in him so he gives me a good price and gets it done quickly."

Dean did laugh then. "Well, that would probably be Jessa."

With a glance at her older sister, Violet said, "I can believe that. She puts the fear of God in me!"

Jessa waved her hand at them. "Oh, go on, you two. I'm not that bad. I expect someone to do their job in a timely fashion and not rip me off. We don't need unethical people working in Collingsworth."

"You're right about that," Dean agreed. "You certainly make my job easier by...encouraging the shady characters to leave town." His radio squawked, drawing his attention from the women. "Well, they're calling my name. I'd better go."

"Thanks for stopping by, Sheriff," Violet said with a smile as she handed his phone back to him.

"Dean. Hopefully we've had our one and only encounter as law enforcement and law breaker."

"Yes, I certainly hope so."

Dean turned to go and then swung back around. "Let me say again how sorry I am for your loss. Julia was a unique woman whom I respected and admired. The town will certainly miss her."

"Thank you, Dean," Jessa said. "I guess we'll see you at

the funeral."

"That you will." Dean tipped his hat. "You ladies have a good day."

He got into his car and pulled it past Violet's, following the curve of the circular driveway to the turn that blocked his view of the women.

Dean had to admit he'd found the interactions between Violet and Jessa interesting. He'd known Jessa since he'd moved to town. Julia Collingsworth had been instrumental in getting him the job of deputy sheriff initially and then the elected position of sheriff later on. Jessa had often been with the older woman when he'd met with her. Those two had been a force to be reckoned with. He wondered if Jessa felt a little lost now that she was basically on her own, not just as the only Collingsworth adult in town, but also as a mother to the two youngest sisters.

He could see that Violet loved her sister and didn't appear to go out of her way to butt heads with her. Jessa had alluded to difficult relationships with her sisters over the years, and Dean had just assumed it was with all of them, but something told him that wasn't the fact with Violet. Though he knew Violet was likely only in town for the funeral, Dean found himself wanting to get to know her better. Definitely not a good idea though. He'd have to remind himself of that in the days ahead.

§◦◦§

"Wow. You must have made an impression on the sheriff during that stop."

Violet glanced over at her sister as she handed one of her bags to Lily. "What?"

"I know Dean well enough that he could have just phoned me with the information," Jessa said. "Instead, he drove all the way out here to talk to you."

"It wasn't my intention to make any kind of impression on anyone." Rose took the small bag Violet held out to her. "Believe me, the last thing I want to do is make an impression on a guy. Particularly a guy living here." She rounded the car to get her laptop bag and camera case from the passenger seat. "But just so we're clear, you're not interested in him, are you?"

Jessa shook her head. "He's a nice guy, but a little too short for my liking."

Violet laughed. "Judging a man on his height? Not nice, Jessa."

Jessa gave her a light smack on the arm as she walked past. "Well, that's one reason. But there was also no spark for me or him apparently, as he's never made any kind of move on me. We're just friends."

"Hope he doesn't mind another Collingsworth friend, because that's all he's gonna get."

Violet led the way back into the house and up the stairs to the room that had been hers during her years at Collingsworth.

"Just set those on the floor," Violet told the girls about the bags they carried. "I'm going to take a nice hot shower. The place I stayed last night was kind of nasty, so I steered clear of the shower. I'll be down in a bit."

Alone in the room, Violet looked around, not too surprised to see that precious little had changed since the last time she'd set foot in it. Not wanting to dwell on the past, Violet hefted one of the bags onto the bed and unzipped it. She pulled out some fresh clothes and then headed for the bathroom that her room shared with the bedroom Laurel would most likely stay in when she arrived.

The manor had a total of ten bedrooms, so they'd never had to share when they'd all lived in the house. Perhaps it would have been better if they had been made to share rooms. Separate rooms had led to private teenage thoughts and then detached adult lives. Violet wanted to believe that this time all home together, without the overbearing presence of their grandmother, might help to draw them closer to each other. But she wasn't holding her breath.

After her shower, Violet made the call to the mechanic

and then headed down to the kitchen, laptop and camera in hand. She rarely went anywhere without one or both of them. Her hair was still damp, and she had chosen a soft flannel long-sleeved shirt over a white tank top and black leggings. Her thick socks slipped a bit on the polished wooden steps, and she couldn't help but do a little slide when she reached the main floor.

"Gran would have told you not to do that," a young voice informed her.

Violet turned to see Rose standing in the doorway to the front room. She smiled at the young girl. "I know. She used to tell me not to do it all the time. But I'll confess...I did it anyway."

Rose's large blue eyes regarded her seriously for a moment before suddenly breaking into a grin. She giggled and then said, "Me too."

Violet was relieved to see the young girl wasn't too distraught over the events of the past few days. She was no doubt upset by her grandmother's death, but Violet was pretty sure the relationship she'd shared with the older woman had not been any closer than the ones her sisters had had with her. Jessa had probably been more active in raising the girls than Gran had.

"Is Jessa in the kitchen?"

Rose nodded. "I think she's making supper."

"I need the password for the internet so I can use my laptop," Violet said as Rose led the way into the kitchen.

Jessa looked up from the pot she was stirring on the stove. "It's on that pink paper over there."

"I'll get it for you," Rose said and did a little skip over to the wall where a bulletin board hung.

Violet settled herself on one of the high stools on the opposite side of the counter from where Jessa worked. "Smells good."

"Hopefully it tastes good too. I'm hoping Laurel wants to cook while she's here. I only do it out of necessity."

"So she's supposed to arrive tonight?" Violet asked as she took the pink slip of paper from Rose and opened her laptop. It didn't take long for her to connect her laptop to the internet.

"Yes. She had to teach today so wouldn't be able to get away until the school day was done. I figure she'll be here around nine."

"Is Matt coming with her?" Violet clicked to open her email, hoping to find something in her inbox from her editor.

"As far as I know," Jessa said as she placed a stack of plates on the counter. "Can you set, sweetie?"

"Sure," Rose replied and picked up the plates and took them to the table in the breakfast nook.

"Has Laurel been here recently?"

"Nope. The last time I saw her was when I took Gran down to Minneapolis for some tests last year." Jessa put the ingredients for a salad on the counter along with a bowl.

Having seen nothing pressing in her email, Violet pulled the salad fixings and bowl closer and began to cut up the vegetables. "I haven't seen her in forever, but I try to call her at least once a month."

"Like you do with me?" Jessa asked, leaning a hip against the counter.

"Yes, I tried to call one of you a week. And if I was feeling particularly brave, I'd give Gran a call too."

Jessa tilted her head to the side, her brow furrowed. "You called Gran? She never told me."

"I did. Not as frequently as I should have, but in spite of our differences, I couldn't ignore the fact that she took us in when we needed someone to take care of us."

"Well, that explains why she hardly ever said anything about you. I heard plenty about how ungrateful Laurel and Cami were, but never you."

"They have their reasons, Jess." Violet began to shred the lettuce. "They were old enough to know that their mom was suddenly gone from their life, but were too young to understand why."

Jessa pushed away from the counter and went to the stove. Violet gave a silent sigh. She loved her sisters—all of them—but she knew Jessa often felt that of the older sisters, it was her against Violet, Laurel and Cami. Violet couldn't blame her for feeling that way, but it was never her intention to side against Jessa. She just wanted to help her understand why the other two felt the way they did.

"Jessa?" Violet glanced to the doorway and saw Lily standing there.

"Yep, sweetie?"

Lily clasped her hands at her waist. "Would it be alright if I went to youth group tonight?"

"Sure, that would be fine. Did you think I'd say no?"

Lily shrugged. "I just didn't know if it was the right thing to do. What with Gran being gone and all."

"I know, but I think it's important you keep doing what feels right. If being with your friends will make you feel better, then you should go."

Lily smiled. "Thanks."

"You have time to eat before you leave, right?"

"Yes. What can I do to help?"

Over their meal, Violet got caught up on everything that was happening in Rose and Lily's lives. She was glad to hear they had lots of interests and friends. Thanks to Jessa, they would probably have the least screwed up lives out of all of them.

After they cleaned up, Lily left in Jessa's car for town. Rose, with a little bit of pouting, was taken to practice her piano under Jessa's supervision. And a bit later she was ushered off to bed, though she protested greatly.

"Can't I stay up to see Laurel?" Rose asked after she'd changed into pajamas and brushed her teeth.

"You can see her in the morning," Jessa said firmly. "We've got a busy few days coming up, and I want you to get your sleep so I don't have to deal with a cranky Rosie."

The little girl's shoulders slumped, but after kissing Violet goodnight, followed Jessa to her bedroom without complaint. In the quiet of the kitchen, Violet rested her head on her hands and sent up a prayer for peace and harmony among the sisters. And patience and wisdom in dealing with them.

Jessa was still upstairs when Violet heard the front door open. She stood and walked into the foyer, grinning when she saw Laurel standing there with a bag in her hand.

"Hey!" Violet quickly crossed to where her sister stood and flung her arms around her. Laurel dropped her bag and returned the embrace.

"It's so good to see you," Violet said as they stepped out of the embrace. "You look great."

"Not as great as you do," Laurel replied with a smile that didn't quite reach her eyes.

Violet noticed then that her younger sister had dark circles beneath her eyes, barely hidden by the makeup she wore. "You been sick?"

"I was a few weeks ago. I think I still haven't quite recovered. I'm on antibiotics for the second time. It's drained me of all my energy, and I still don't have it back." She brushed a hand across her forehead, pushing aside her blonde hair. "Just getting ready to come here zapped me."

"Well, you gonna say hi to me?" a husky voice asked from behind Laurel.

❧ Chapter Three ❧

VIOLET'S jaw dropped as she took in the tall, leggy blonde standing in the doorway.

"Cami! We didn't know you were arriving tonight too. This is great!" Violet moved past Laurel to give Cami a hug. As soon as she got close, she caught the scent of cigarette smoke. She groaned inwardly as she imagined what Jessa would have to say about that.

"How are you doing?" Violet asked after she gave her a quick hug.

Cami shrugged. "I've been worse."

Cami had height like Jessa, but her hair was blond like Laurel's. And while Jessa tended more toward loose, flowing dresses and skirts, Cami's present outfit ended a good five inches above her knees and showed off every curve the girl had.

Violet had a feeling this was not going to go well. Both girls looked braced for war. "Let me go get Jessa. She's upstairs putting Rose to bed."

"We'll get the rest of our stuff while you do that," Laurel said.

Hoping to have a minute to talk with Jessa before they came back down, Violet took the stairs to the second floor two at a time. She saw her older sister coming out of her own bedroom.

"Hey, Jess. Listen, Laurel just arrived."

Jessa smiled. "That's great. She made good time."

As Jessa moved to go past Violet to the stairs, Violet laid a hand on her arm. "Um, she's not alone."

"Did Matt come with her?"

Violet shook her head. "Not Matt. Cami."

"Cami's here?" A frown creased Jessa's brow.

"Yes, Cami's here. And..."

"And what?"

"Well, let's just say there are a few things about her that will no doubt tempt you to comment. I'm asking you to please, at least for tonight, not say anything."

Jessa glanced toward the stairs. "What are you talking about?"

"She's wearing an outfit that would probably make Gran turn in her grave." Violet paused. "And she smells like cigarette smoke."

Jessa let out a long breath. "You're determined to play peacekeeper again, aren't you?"

"For Gran's sake, we need to do our best to get along. We have more important things to focus on than what Cami's wearing and the fact that she smokes."

Jessa didn't say anything for a long moment, but then nodded. "For tonight, at least. No promises beyond that. I will try my best to keep my comments under control, but if she doesn't do the same..."

Violet nodded. "I understand. I'm just asking that you try."

"I'll try."

Jessa turned and headed down the stairs. Violet stood

there for a minute praying for peace. By the time she got to the foyer, Jessa was greeting the other two girls. All seemed well for the time being. Violet knew better than to expect it to last too long, but she could always hope.

By the next afternoon, Violet was ready for an escape from the tension in the house. She had tried to keep the peace between the three sisters, but now she was going to let them have at it without her there to keep things calm.

She didn't even bother to tell any of them she was leaving. They were too caught up in their drama to miss her anyway. Thankfully Lily had taken Rose to spend the afternoon with friends, so they had been spared the snide comments, thinly veiled barbs and outright arguments.

Not sure where to go, Violet eventually found herself in front of the sheriff's office. She wondered if this was where Dean worked. If it was, and if he was in, she had a few questions for him. She'd planned to ask him after the funeral, but if he was here on a Saturday, she'd take it as a sign that now was a good time.

A uniformed deputy sitting behind a desk looked up as she walked in. He stood and approached the counter that separated them. "What can I do for you?"

"I'm wondering if the Sheriff works here."

The deputy nodded. "Yep, he does."

"Does he happen to be in today?"

"As a matter of fact, he came in just a bit ago."

"Would you ask him if he has a few minutes to talk with me?"

"And you are?"

"Violet."

The man smiled at her. "Got a last name, Miss Violet?"

Violet sighed. "Collingsworth."

The man's brows raised a fraction. "I'm sure he'll have time for you. I'll be right back."

While she knew that Cami enjoyed the prestige their last name brought in this town, Violet didn't care for it. By appearance, she fit in the least with the sisters and had been able to fly below the radar when meeting people for the first time. Her mother had never told her for sure what nationality her father had been, but it was a pretty good guess that he'd been Hispanic or perhaps Asian. People that didn't know the circumstances of the sisters' births were usually pretty surprised when she identified herself as a Collingsworth.

The deputy returned quickly with Dean following behind him. He was out of uniform, and for the first time, she got a good look at him without his hat. He wore a black turtleneck shirt tucked into a pair of black jeans. He had a bit of a five o'clock shadow that, along with his dark hair and attire, gave him a dangerous air. Violet had been known to go for something just for the thrill of the danger it posed. But she was pretty sure that where this man was concerned, that was not a good thing.

He gave her a smile. "I didn't expect to see you here today."

"Yeah, I hadn't planned on heading into town, but my other sisters arrived last night and things are a bit tense at the manor. I needed a break."

"Sorry to hear that. Is there something I can help you with? Shane said you wanted to speak with me about something?"

"Yes, I have a favor to ask regarding my family."

Dean tilted his head. "Need me to arrest one or more of them?"

"Only if you can do it for disturbing my peace of mind."

Dean laughed and shook his head. "Sorry. No can do."

"Bummer," Violet said with a smile. Already she could feel some of the tension easing from her neck. "I do have something I'd like to speak to you about though, if you have a couple of minutes."

"Sure. C'mon in." Dean opened the gate that allowed her past the counter. He led the way to his office and shut the door behind her. His office had glass windows so the closed door gave them privacy to talk, but they were still visible to the rest of the office. He motioned to a chair and then sat down at his desk. "So what's on your mind?"

Violet settled into the vinyl covered chair, resting her elbows on the wooden arm rests and lacing her fingers together. As she looked across the desk to where Dean sat, she suddenly wished she'd taken a bit more time with her appearance that morning. Jeans, another flannel shirt and tank top with her hair in a ponytail didn't exactly give a great impression. Too late now, Violet thought as she shifted in her seat.

"How much do you know about the history of my family? My sisters and I?"

Dean didn't answer right away. Then he leaned forward and braced his arms on his desk. "Well, your grandmother told me a little bit. And, of course, there are plenty of rumors floating around town."

Violet nodded. "Yes, I've heard the rumors. They all hold a bit of truth." She bit her lip. "I'm wondering if you'd be able to help me find my mom."

Dean's brows rose, his blue eyes widening. "You don't know where she is?"

"No, we haven't seen or heard from her since she dropped Lily off just after she was born."

"Lily?" Dean asked. "Don't you mean Rose?

Violet stared at Dean, trying to decide how much to trust him. She sensed he wasn't a man given to spreading stories, and if he was going to help her, it stood to reason he needed to know everything.

"No, I mean Lily. Rose isn't my sister. She's my niece."

Dean's jaw dropped slightly, but he snapped it shut before saying, "So one of your sisters is her mother?"

"Yes, but rather than have rumors about another

pregnant teen on her hands, Gran decided to pass Rose off as another daughter of my mom's."

"Which sister?"

Violet had known that question would most likely follow the revelation of Rose's parentage. She sighed and shook her head. "It's not my place to reveal that information. All I can say is she's not my daughter."

"Does Rose know about this?"

"Not that I'm aware of. Gran was pretty adamant about keeping that secret within the family. But who knows now that she's gone. I think that will be up to my sister on whether or not she wants to tell her." Violet clasped her hands in her lap. "So do you think you can help me out?"

Dean's shoulders slumped, and his gaze dropped. He didn't say anything for several moments. When he looked back up and met her gaze, Violet read regret there even before he said the words.

"I'm sorry. I can't."

Disappointment swamped Violet. She had so hoped he'd be able to help her with this since she really didn't know where to start on her own. "Do you mind if I ask why?"

"I made a promise to your grandmother that I would never help you look for your mother."

His explanation left Violet speechless...for a few seconds. "What?"

"I really didn't think it would be a big deal. She came to see me a few months back and asked me to promise that should any of you ladies come to me that I wouldn't help you find your mother or what happened to her." Dean shrugged. "If I had known..."

"I know she didn't like us even talking about her, but I didn't think she'd go this far." Violet leaned forward. "I don't suppose it makes any difference that she's gone?"

Dean shook his head. "I like to think I'm a man of my word. And I gave your grandmother my word. However..." He leaned back in his chair, a thoughtful expression on his face. "That being said, I might be able to point you in the direction of someone who could help you."

Violet straightened, hope flowing through her once again. "Would you do that?"

Dean nodded. "I know a guy who loves stuff like this. I'll have to give him a call first before I promise anything for sure though. Are your sisters on board with this as well?"

She sighed. "No. I haven't told them what I'm doing. Jessa will no doubt object flat out. The other two...I don't know."

"So why are you wanting to find her?" Dean asked. "It seems very important to you."

"It is. Of all of us, I was the one who was with her the longest. I probably have the clearest memories of her as a mother."

"How old were you when she brought you to Collingsworth?"

"I had just turned six. Laurel was three and Cami was almost two. She dropped the three of us off together. Mama left Jessa when she was just days old so she has no connection at all with her. Same with Lily. Unfortunately, Laurel and Cami have no real memories of her either, since they were so young. Though to be honest, memories of that time might not have been the best thing for them."

"And yet you have them," Dean pointed out.

"Yes, I do. And it took me a long time to be able to relegate them to the past, reminding myself that our mother was not a well person mentally. I think that's why I don't have the issues with Gran that Laurel and Cami do. I know just what she rescued us from. And no matter how stern or strict she was with us, it was better than what was happening to us with our mom."

Dean's brows drew together. Violet thought he might ask for details, but all he said was, "So why do you want to find her now?"

"It's been on my mind for a while. I've made some casual

inquiries using information I had on where she was right before she dropped us off, but it's all led to dead ends. I just want to make sure she's okay."

Dean nodded. "All right, I'll give my friend a call and see if he's able to help you."

"Thank you."

"I wish I could do more."

"I understand why you can't. Knowing Gran, she probably would have found a way to haunt you if you broke your promise to her." Violet grinned.

Dean chuckled. "Yes, if anyone could do that it would be Julia Collingsworth."

Silence stretched between them until Violet stood. Dean followed her lead.

"I'll let you get back to your Saturday," she said. "Thanks again."

"You heading back to the manor?" Dean asked as he rounded the desk and opened the door for her.

Violet sighed. "Yes. I suppose I'd better get back there and make sure everyone is still alive."

"So the funeral is tomorrow afternoon?" Dean led the way out into the main area again.

"Yes. Although from what Jessa says, it's more of a memorial service. Gran didn't want people staring at her dead body, so we'll have a private family viewing and burial on Monday."

"I heard that she requested her body go to a funeral home in a neighboring town."

Violet gave a short laugh. "Yeah. She said there was no way that anyone she'd spent her life looking in the eye would be seeing her naked body."

"Sounds like Julia."

"Yep. She was quite a woman. Should be interesting to see what her will holds. I have a feeling she didn't make it simple and straightforward."

"I kinda hope she did for the sake of you and your sisters. It doesn't sound like more complications are what your relationships need."

"You can say that again." Violet leaned against the glass door at the front of the office and pushed it open. A rush of cool air greeted her. "Well, thanks again. Guess I'll see you tomorrow."

Dean nodded. "I'll be there."

Violet stepped through the door and let it close behind her. She headed to where she'd parked her car. Once inside she started it up and sat for a few minutes trying to convince herself that she really wanted to return to the manor. She loved her sisters, she really did, but after this morning, she didn't like any of the older ones very much. But she figured she needed to get back to at least keep too much of the emotional strife from effecting the two youngest if they were back from town.

∾∾

Dean stood at the window of the office watching as Violet climbed into her old car. He'd been surprised when the deputy had said who was there to see him. He hadn't planned to be in the office that day, but had come into town to drop Addy off at a birthday party and had figured he'd just hang around until it was pick up time.

How he wished he'd been able to give Violet the help she'd asked of him. But the stern words of the Collingsworth matriarch that day in his office a few months ago had held him back.

She'd stuck a finger directly at him, her steely gaze fierce. "You'd better keep your word, young man. I'm counting on you helping me spare my girls from more heart ache. They've had plenty already and no doubt more is on the way. But don't let it be from you."

Dean had made the promise easily, never imagining that not long after that conversation he'd have a beautiful young woman come and ask him to help her with the one thing he couldn't. He felt like he'd let her down and for some reason that really bothered him. The least he could do was see if he could find someone who could help her.

Being a single man in a town like Collingsworth, he'd been at the center of his share of matchmaking. And yet none had drawn his interest the way Violet Collingsworth had. He wondered what Julia would think about that. He wasn't even sure what he thought of it. His focus the last few years had been on picking up the pieces of his shattered life and moving forward.

The memories didn't come as frequently now. The sound of gunshots outside his home. The screams of his sister. The cries of her young daughter. And his own anguished sobs as he bent over the body of his twin sister, his knees pressing into the blood soaked carpet as he tried to stop the flow of life from her wounded body. But his efforts had been in vain, and when the emergency crews arrived, they'd had to forcibly remove him from his sister's side. Blindly he'd reached for his two year old niece, holding her close as he tried to gather himself back together.

⚡ Chapter Four ⚡

IT had been his fault. After his divorce, he'd thrown himself even more into his work as a detective on the Minneapolis Police force. He'd worked some important cases, but after having his cover blown on a case and almost losing his life, he'd moved into a more supervisory role. It had taken a while, but one of the cases he'd previously investigated had finally gone to trial. He'd been preparing to testify in the well-publicized trial that had huge ramifications for some people in political offices. He'd brushed off the need for any sort of police protection; after all, he was police. But he hadn't been able to protect his sister. She had moved in with him a year earlier when her husband's suicide left her with a young child and no way to support herself. They'd both been getting back on their feet when the drive-by shooting had changed everything.

His focus in the months following the shooting had been Adelaide and what was best for her. Why Julia Collingsworth had contacted him out of the blue one day was a mystery to him. His lawyer had passed on her information to him, saying that she had a proposal for him. Within the month, he and Adelaide were on their way to the town of

Collingsworth. It wasn't as far away from Minneapolis as he might have liked, but he had peace about the move. It had felt like a God-given opportunity.

Things were finally going well for him and the now six-year old Adelaide. She enjoyed school, loved her friends and was thriving in a way that he could only have dreamed possible. He had a nice rustic home a couple of miles out of town that suited him just fine. And now Violet Collingsworth had walked into his life. She was the first woman to really interest him in years. Unfortunately, thanks to Jessa and Julia, he knew all about her wandering lifestyle. He wasn't sure she'd be interested in someone so firmly rooted in a town she'd apparently been eager to escape years ago. And then add a child to that mix, and she may very well run in the opposite direction.

He watched as her car backed into the street and headed out of his sight. Dean sighed and turned back to his desk. As he'd listened to Violet share revelations about her family, he wondered just how much more Julia had manipulated and controlled, not just for her family, but for the town of Collingsworth. He was pretty sure if it hadn't been for her support, he wouldn't have this position. She'd called a town council meeting to reveal his past qualifications in private due to the nature of his sister's death. Once she'd publicly made it known that she backed him for the job of sheriff, no one else had put their name in the hat. It hadn't sat completely well with him, but he'd been desperate enough for security and stability for himself and Addy that he'd gone along with it. However, another election was coming up, and Julia wouldn't be there to steer the vote. He could only hope he'd done a good enough job that people would now vote for him based on his own merits.

His phone chirped an alarm to remind him to pick up Addy. Pushing aside the thoughts of Violet, he retrieved his jacket and left the building. He would have to deal with Violet's situation later.

※

Although the air was filled with the wonderful aroma of something baking, the manor was suspiciously quiet when Violet walked in. Glancing around for any signs of carnage, she made her way to the kitchen. She paused when she spotted Laurel there with the two younger girls.

"Smells good," Violet said.

The three looked toward her. Rose and Lily gave her big smiles. Laurel's was a bit more reserved, and she still looked tired.

Violet joined them at the counter. "Where are Jessa and Cami?"

"Jessa's out in the greenhouse," Lily said.

"And I think Cami's upstairs taking a nap or something," Laurel added.

Violet met Laurel's gaze. "Everything okay?"

"Depends what you mean by everything." Laurel took the cookie sheet they'd been working on to the oven and slid it in. "Jessa and Cami aren't talking to each other. And I'm too tired to deal with their cr-" She glanced at the younger girls. "With their issues."

Lily grabbed Rose's hand. "Why don't we go tell Jessa that Violet's back?"

Once the girls had left the kitchen, Violet said, "What's going on with you, Laurel? You just aren't yourself."

"I had a bad case of the flu a few weeks back and then a got a throat infection right after. I just can't seem to get back to normal. I have no energy. If I could, I'd sleep twenty-four hours a day."

"I'm sorry to hear that. You should be taking it easy while you're here. You don't have to be doing all this," Violet said and waved her hand at the cookies already cooling on racks.

"Cooking and baking are what I enjoy." Laurel leaned against the counter and picked up a cookie. Handing it to Violet she said, "I am glad to see you. In spite of the circumstances."

Violet broke the cookie and popped a small piece into her

mouth. "I'm glad to see you too. How is Matt?"

"He's doing okay. A bit frustrated with me though. The weekend comes now, and all I want to do is curl up on the couch and sleep. We used to do stuff all the time, but the past few weekends, he eventually just goes out on his own."

Concern for her sister and her marriage grew within Violet. The last thing she needed was more stress with the situation in Collingsworth. "Is he coming for the funeral?"

"He said he would." Laurel shrugged. "We'll see."

"So you decided to come back?" Jessa asked as she walked in, a basket in her hand. She set it on the counter and braced her hands on her hips, glaring at Violet. "You're a chicken."

Violet nodded. "You betcha. Besides, you're both old enough now that you shouldn't need me to mediate all your fights."

"She's stubborn," Jessa said flatly. She began to empty the contents of the basket into the sink and wash them.

"So are you." Violet popped the last of the cookie in her mouth. "What are you disagreeing about now?"

"Everything." Jessa handed several tomatoes to Laurel. "Will those be okay?"

"They're lovely. The sauce will be perfect with them being so fresh."

Jessa turned her attention back to Violet. "I don't like how she dresses around the younger girls. Gran and I have worked hard to instill the importance of modesty in Rose and Lily. I don't need them to look at Cami and figure it's okay to dress so provocatively. And then there's her smoking."

"I understand that. But Rose and Lily need to understand that not everyone in the world lives according Gran's guidelines. They need to understand for themselves how important it is and not be judgmental of others. Cami is not in the same place spiritually as us. We can't hold her to those standards."

"So we're just supposed to accept that she's dressing like

a....streetwalker?"

Violet sighed. "No. I'll talk to her, but I make no promises. As you said, she is stubborn."

And that stubbornness played itself out after supper when Cami informed them she was going into town to go to the bar.

"And just how are you going to get there?" Jessa asked.

Cami's short laugh had an edge to it. "You think I'd come to this backwoods town without a way to escape? The car we came in is one I rented."

Jessa glanced at Laurel who nodded. "I was too tired to want to drive my car up. I figured I could get a ride back with Matt if she left before I did."

Cami crossed her arms and smiled at Jessa. "Any other objections?"

"Back off." Violet laid a hand on Cami's arm. "Go ahead, if you have to, but please don't drink and drive. If you have more than one drink, give me a call when you want to come home."

"Why are you enabling her?" Jessa demanded, her green eyes flashing.

"I'm not enabling her. She's an adult, and she's going to do this whether we want her to or not. I'm just trying to keep her and others safe."

Jessa turned on her heel and left the room. Laurel sighed and sank down on the stool next to the counter. "Do you have to antagonize her so much, Cam?"

Cami flipped her hair over her shoulder. "She asks for it, coming off all holier than thou."

Violet wondered if the too short, too tight outfit Cami wore was really her normal attire, or if she'd gone shopping for a new wardrobe designed specifically to tick Jessa off. "Well, you're an adult so if you want to go, we can't stop you, but I'm serious about driving. You drive drunk, I personally will call the sheriff on you. Do not do anything stupid."

"Oh, haven't you heard? Stupid is my middle name." With

one last glare in the direction Jessa had disappeared, Cami headed for the door.

"I'm going to take a shower and go to bed," Laurel said when it was just her and Violet.

"Can I get you anything? Tea? Milk? Hot chocolate?"

Laurel paused, obviously tempted. "Hot chocolate?"

Violet smiled. "I'll come up in about half an hour, okay?"

Laurel nodded and headed for the stairs.

"Did she go?" Jessa came into the kitchen from the back yard

"Yes, she did." Violet took two mugs out of the cupboard. "Want some hot chocolate? I'm making some for myself and Laurel. I was going to see if Lily and Rose wanted some too."

Jessa stood there, hands clenched at her sides, but then just seemed to deflate as if all the fight had gone out of her. Her head dropped forward. "I don't mean to be so...rigid. I know that's what pushed you guys away from Gran. I don't want that to happen to us. I wish I could be more like you."

Violet rested a hand on her chest. "Like me?"

"You seem to be able to deal with all of us without getting uptight and frustrated."

"I've been having to deal since I was really young. And I've also come to realize that some battles are more important to fight than others."

Jessa took a deep breath then said, "Yes, I'll have some hot chocolate. And I'll go ask the girls if they want some as well."

All four of them took Laurel's hot chocolate up to her room along with a container of the cookies she'd made earlier. She came out of the bathroom wearing a thick robe, her hair wrapped in a towel. She looked at them in surprise but then joined them, mug cupped in her hands.

Sitting cross legged on the bed with her sisters, Violet felt sad Cami was missing out, but she was glad to see Jessa relaxing and sharing stories from their past and talking about Gran. Even Laurel seemed to come out of her tired funk. The days ahead weren't going to be easy, so Violet was glad for this little bit of time when they could connect over hot chocolate and oatmeal cookies and share memories of the person who had brought them all together in the first place.

§∞♫

Dean looked over at his phone when it rang. It was after eleven, and usually no one called him this late unless it was an emergency. He threw back his covers and sat up, reaching for the phone.

"What's up?" he said having recognized the number of one of his deputies.

"We've got a problem, sir."

Dean stood, making his way to the chair where he'd left his clothes earlier. "What sort of problem?"

"Drunken disturbance."

Dean paused then dropped his jeans back on the chair. "Why are you calling me for a drunken disturbance?"

"Uh, this is kind of a special circumstance, I think. She says she's a Collingsworth."

He grabbed his jeans again. "Which bar?" The deputy told him where they were. "Okay, I'll be there as soon as possible. If you need to, take her to the jail. I'll deal with this."

After hanging up, Dean pulled on his jeans, a pair of socks and a white T-shirt. He probably should have put on his uniform, but he was hoping this would be less of an issue if he didn't show up in an official capacity. He did make sure to have his badge in the pocket of his jacket though.

He hated to do it, but he went to the small cabin next to the house and knocked on the door. When the elderly woman answered it, Dean told her what had happened.

"Can you listen for her?"

"No problem. That's what I'm here for." She took the monitor from him. "I'll make sure she's okay."

"Thanks, Sylvia."

Sylvia Miller had been living in the small cabin next door when he'd moved in and had readily stepped in to help care for Adelaide when his schedule required it. In her younger years, the widowed woman had also worked at the manor for Julia Collingsworth, and her husband had worked as grounds keeper there too. Dean was pretty sure it was just one more thing the older woman had worked out for him.

He took his own vehicle, once again hoping to appear a little less threatening to whoever he was going to be dealing with. Though the officer hadn't given him a name, he was pretty sure it wasn't Jessa or Violet. At least he hoped it wasn't either of them. That would definitely make the situation more complicated.

There were quite a few cars in the parking lot of the bar along with a couple of cruisers. It seemed a bit of overkill given they were just dealing with a drunk. He parked in the first empty spot he could find then went into the bar to try to figure out how to get out of this without dragging the Collingsworth name through the mud.

It took him a minute to adjust to the dark interior. He looked around for his officers and found them standing at the bar, their attention focused on the stage. His eyes widened as his gaze went to where they were looking.

❧ *Chapter Five* ❧

ONE of the classier bars in town, this one had a grand piano in the corner. And right then, a scantily clad blonde was lounging on top of it. Singing. There was no doubting the talent of the woman, but as a man approached the piano, she stopped singing and began to yell and curse at him. Dean was pretty sure now that this was Camilla Collingsworth. From what he'd heard, Laurel was a school teacher and Camilla was a singer.

He moved to where the officers stood. "Have you tried to get her down?"

They straightened when they realized their boss stood next to them. "Oh yes, several times. She fought us like a wild cat the last time we tried. That's when we called you."

Dean took a deep breath and let it out. Slowly he made his way to the piano. He stopped a few feet away, hands on his hips. Her gaze connected with his, and she stopped singing for a moment. He waited for the cursing to begin, but instead she gave him a sultry smile. "Hello, handsome. Do you have a special request?"

He heard the snickering behind him. Everyone in the bar

no doubt knew who he was, even if the blonde didn't. "Why don't you give your voice a rest for a few minutes? You're very talented. I'd hate for you to strain your vocal cords."

She looked at him for a long moment before moving to the edge of the piano and sitting up. Crossing her legs, she began to sing again, this time a slow sexy ballad. Dean waited. After a few minutes, she slid off the piano and walked toward him, still singing. He kept his gaze on her face, knowing that her scantily clad body was something he shouldn't be looking at. She came to a stop in front of him, running a long red fingernail down the front of his T-shirt as her song ended. "Want to take me home, handsome?"

"Yes, actually, I do." Dean took the microphone from her and handed it to the deputy who'd come to stand beside him. He slipped off his jacket and put it around her shoulders. "My car's just outside."

Obviously still unaware that he was an officer of the law, she leaned into him as they walked from the bar. Dean really hoped that she passed out as soon as they got in the car.

"I'm cold," she said as he opened the passenger door for her.

"The car will warm up soon." After making sure she was buckled in, he shut the door.

"These are hers, sir." Dean turned to find a deputy holding out a bundle of clothing. As he took them, he shook his head. He was having a hard time figuring out how this woman could be related to Jessa and Violet.

"I'm just going to take her to the manor without an official report. I think the Collingsworth family has enough to deal with right now."

"Yes, sir. That's why I called you."

"You did well." Dean clapped the young man on the shoulder.

He climbed behind the wheel and saw that Cami had her eyes closed. He turned the heat up because he was also finding a bit chilly without his jacket. He left the parking lot, but then pulled over to the side of the road just outside of town. He took his phone out and tapped Violet's name in his contact list. He'd added her earlier when she'd given him her number. He'd debated phoning Jessa, but from what he'd seen, it was a good guess that Violet would handle this better than her older sister.

"Hello?" Her voice was low and husky like he'd woken her.

"Sorry to call you so late. It's Dean."

There was a beat of silence before she said, "Dean?"

"Yes. I'm calling because we had a little incident in town tonight."

He heard her sigh. "What did Cami do now?"

"Let's just say she gave an impromptu performance that was perhaps just a bit much for our town."

"Where is she? I told her to call me if she drank and needed a ride."

"She's sitting next to me in my car. I'm on my way out to the Manor. My deputies called me when they realized she was a Collingsworth. We're not taking any official steps at this point. Just a warning and dropping her off at home."

"Jessa's going to hit the roof."

"Yeah, I kinda figured she might which is why I called you."

Violet chuckled. "You afraid of her?"

"I wouldn't say afraid...maybe something more like I have a healthy respect for living with all my limbs intact? I felt the same way with your grandmother."

"Yeah, I hear you." He heard the rustle of movement. "Okay, I'll be downstairs to meet you."

"Thanks. See you in a few minutes."

"You're a cop." The words were slurred and slow.

Dean glanced toward the girl slumped in the seat, relieved he couldn't see her too clearly because of the darkness. "Yes, I am. The sheriff, in fact."

"Brought...out...the...big...guns."

"I'm a family friend."

"I could...be...your...friend. I'm a...good...friend."

"I'm sure you are, but let's wait until we've been properly introduced. I'm hoping you don't remember much about this evening."

"Did you...call Jessa?"

"No, I called Violet."

"Good. Jessa is..a...bi-" Her words drifted off.

Again Dean tried to reconcile this girl with the Collingsworths he'd met so far. She clearly had some issues.

It wasn't long before he pulled to a stop in front of the manor. The front door opened as soon as he climbed from the SUV. Violet came out, her arms crossed over her middle. "How is she?"

"Very...friendly."

"I'm so sorry, Dean." Violet walked to the car and opened the door. "C'mon, Cam, you need to come inside."

As Cami slid out of the seat, Violet looked at her then asked, "What is she wearing?"

"Um, my jacket, and I would assume it's her undergarments." He opened the back door and retrieved the bundle he'd tossed there earlier. He handed them to Violet. "I think these are her clothes."

"Good grief." Violet guided Cami up the stairs and into the house. Dean followed, but stopped just outside the door. Violet reappeared a second later and held out his jacket. "Here you go. Thanks for helping her."

"You're welcome. I hope she's okay."

"She'll be fine...if she survives Jessa."

Dean watched Violet disappear into the house. He took a whiff of his jacket and then tossed it into the back seat. The scent of cigarette smoke and Cami's perfume were a bit much for him. He'd rather be cold. Now if Violet had been the one to wear it, he might feel differently.

Drawing his thoughts from that direction, Dean wearily headed for home and bed hoping that now that all the Collingsworth women were safely under one roof, there would be no more emergencies he had to deal with.

ဢ

Anger swelled within Violet as she struggled to get Cami up to her bedroom on the second floor. Her outdoor lifestyle made her fit and strong, but the dead weight of her drunken sister was almost too much. She tried to be as quiet as possible because waking Jessa would no doubt bring down a whole lot of fury on Cami. And while she deserved it, Violet was pretty sure she wouldn't remember a thing the next morning. If Jessa was going to give her a lecture, Violet wanted to make sure the young woman remembered it.

She dragged Cami up into the unmade bed and plopped her against the pillow. Violet couldn't believe what Cami had done. What was going on in that brain of hers that she would do something so unbelievably stupid? Any of the earlier understanding and patience she'd had for her sister had disappeared. She'd just gone and proved Jessa right.

Violet tugged the blanket over Cami and shut the light off as she walked out of the room. She had to leave before she tried to slap or shake some sense into the passed out girl. Outside in the hall, she took a deep breath and exhaled.

While it had been nice to see Dean again, the circumstances had been less than ideal. It was embarrassing to think of him seeing her sister that way. And who knew what Cami had said before passing out. Dean was an attractive man, and Cami was known to flirt. And with alcohol in her system...

She wished she could just keep the evening's events from Jessa, but Violet had a feeling she'd find out regardless. Turning, she went to Jessa's door and knocked.

"Come in."

Violet pushed open the door and saw that Jessa was sitting in her bed, a book in her lap and music playing softly.

"Can we talk for a minute?"

"Sure. Come sit."

Violet plunked down on the bed beside Jessa. "So, I figure I'd better be the one to tell you that Cami got into a bit of trouble tonight."

Jessa sighed. "What happened?"

"I got a call from Dean that he was bringing her home. Apparently she decided to perform on top of the bar's piano in nothing but her underwear."

Jessa's jaw dropped. Her eyes closed briefly and when she met Violet's gaze again, her expression held only sadness and disappointment. "I don't understand. I really don't."

"Well, in this case, I'm with you. I expected she'd get drunk, and I'd have to go pick her up. I never dreamed she'd go so far that the bar would have to call in the cops. Thankfully they called Dean to deal with her instead of hauling her off to jail."

"And I guess he called you because he knew I'd hit the roof."

Violet shrugged. "But I figured I should let you know before tomorrow. I'm sorry to say that in this day and age, there are probably more than a few videos of it floating around."

Jessa shuddered. "I guess that will be her burden to bear. I'm trying really hard to remind myself she's an adult and is responsible for these decisions, not me. And her actions are not a reflection on me."

Violet nodded. "I agree, but I'm worried and a bit scared. She could have ended up in a lot more trouble tonight had people not recognized who she was, and looked out for her. In her inebriated state she probably would have gone home with anyone who suggested it to her."

"Do I need to talk to her tomorrow or just let you handle it? You seem better able to deal with her than I do."

"Let's just see how it unfolds. I doubt she'll be up to go to church with us and then we've got Gran's memorial service in the afternoon. That's what we need to be focused on right now, not Cami and her antics." Violet saw Jessa's head dip. She laid her hand on her sister's. "Are you doing okay?"

Jessa looked up. "Yes. I'm fine. I just need to get through the next couple of days, and then I'll take the time I need to grieve. I just can't do it when there's so much that needs my attention."

"Well, let me know what you need me to do. I will try and run interference with you and Cami. Don't even let her worry you right now. I only told you about what happened tonight because I figured it's going to be getting around town and didn't want you to be the last to know."

"Thanks. I think." Jessa gave her a weak smile, brushing back an errant red curl. "This too shall pass."

"Yes, it shall." Violet hugged her, and then crawled off the bed. "See you in the morning. Church is still at eleven?"

"Yep. Sunday school is at 9:30, but I probably won't go for that tomorrow."

After saying goodnight, Violet returned to her own room. She put her pajamas back on and crawled into the bed she'd left when Dean had called. Flopping back on her pillow she stared up at the darkness. She'd known when the call had come that Gran had passed she'd have to deal with all the relationship issues; she just hadn't known how bad it would be with Cami.

She curled onto her side, closed her eyes and prayed for wisdom and guidance. And protection for a sister who seemed determined to wreck her life.

~ Chapter Six ~

DEAN spotted a much more subdued looking Cami Collingsworth at her sister's side the next day at the memorial service. He'd seen Violet at a distance that morning at church, but there had been no sign of Cami. Because he'd had Addy with him, he hadn't approached her. He didn't want Addy to get any ideas, and he wasn't sure he was ready for Violet to know he was a single dad just yet.

The six sisters made a striking group as they walked with the pastor of their church to the front of the arena where the service was being held. The large building had been the only place they figured would be big enough to hold everyone who was likely to come. Since it was on a Sunday afternoon, a lot of people would be able to attend who might not have been able to on a weekday. He suspected quite a few had come up from Minneapolis as well as surrounding towns.

The sisters all wore white, and Dean wondered if it had been a request of Julia's. He knew from talking to Jessa that the service had been planned by Julia well in advance of her death. Control...it had all been about control with that woman. And something told him she wasn't done controlling the lives of her family members.

He hoped he'd be able to have a word with Violet once the service was over to make sure everything was okay after the events of the previous night. That had definitely not been what the sisters had needed, but hopefully Cami would behave herself now for Jessa and Violet's sake.

Dressed in his formal sheriff's uniform, Dean made his way down the side aisle to the place the pastor had reserved for him. According to Julia's wishes, he was to read some Scripture and pray. He would gladly do that for her after all she'd done for him.

Addy had opted to go to a friend's house rather than come to the service. The girl's mother had offered to watch her since she wasn't able to attend anyway because of her other children and lack of childcare. He glanced down the row to where Violet sat, Cami on one side, Lily on the other. She caught his gaze and smiled. He returned it, glad to see that she didn't appear too stressed.

The white dress she wore highlighted her dark hair and tanned skin. This was the first time he'd seen her hair down, and it was longer than he'd realized. When she bent forward to say something to someone further down the row, it slid like silk across her back. He wondered what it would feel like to touch it...run his fingers through it.

The thought caught Dean by surprise. It had been a while since he'd last felt himself drawn to a woman in that way. It had just seemed easier, and somewhat necessary with Addy, to steer clear of that sort of attraction. But there was something about her that captured his attention on more levels than he was used to or wanted.

He turned his attention to the stage that had been set up at the north end of the arena as the pastor climbed the stairs. There was an abundance of flowers on the sides of the stage, and a large easel with a framed portrait of Julia Collingsworth stood next to the podium. He stared at the picture, remembering his last few interactions with her. She'd still managed to look as put together as ever, but looking back now he could see there had been a frailness to her that had never been there before. It was only in the last couple of weeks she had finally let people know how sick she really was. From talking to Jessa, Dean knew Julia had kept it a secret from even those closest to her.

Dean stood when he heard the pastor call him to the front. Bible in hand, he climbed to the podium. He laid it down, open to the passage he'd bookmarked earlier. He braced his hands on the smooth wood and looked out at the expanse of people there.

"Julia Collingsworth was quite a woman. She came into my life after I'd gone through a tragedy that left me a broken man. I don't know why God sent her my way, but to this day I'm eternally grateful to her and to God for the opportunity she gave me. She was a woman with high expectations of those around her, but she held no one to a higher expectation than she had for herself. And I know there was a soft side to her that many of us saw and were blessed by." Dean cleared his throat. "She chose to have me read Psalm 103 today."

He paused and then began to read the Scripture verses.

"Bless the Lord, O my soul;
and all that is within me,
bless His holy name!
Bless the Lord, O my soul,
and forget not all His benefits:
Who forgives all your iniquities,
who heals all your diseases,
Who redeems your life from destruction,
Who crowns you with loving kindness
and tender mercies,
Who satisfies your mouth with good things,
so that your youth is renewed like the eagle's.
The Lord executes righteousness,
and justice for all who are oppressed.
He made known His ways to Moses,
His acts to the children of Israel.

The Lord is merciful and gracious,
slow to anger, and abounding in mercy.
He will not always strive with us,
nor will He keep His anger forever.
He has not dealt with us according to our sins,
nor punished us according to our iniquities.
For as the heavens are high above the earth,
So great is His mercy toward those who fear Him;
As far as the east is from the west,
so far has He removed our transgressions from us.
As a father pities his children,
so the Lord pities those who fear Him.
For He knows our frame;
He remembers that we are dust.
As for man, his days are like grass;
as a flower of the field, so he flourishes.
For the wind passes over it,
and it is gone, and its place remembers it no more.
But the mercy of the Lord is from everlasting
to everlasting on those who fear Him,
And His righteousness to children's children,
To such as keep His covenant, and to those who
remember His commandments to do them.
The Lord has established His throne in heaven,
and His kingdom rules over all.
Bless the Lord, you His angels,
who excel in strength, who do His word,
Heeding the voice of His word.
Bless the Lord, all you His hosts,
you ministers of His, who do His pleasure.
Bless the Lord, all His works,

in all places of His dominion.
Bless the Lord, O my soul!"

When he finished the Bible reading, Dean said a brief prayer, asking for comfort for the family during their time of grief. After completing his role in the service, Dean returned to his seat. He wondered if any of the sisters would get up to speak. The program didn't say anything specifically about them participating, but near the end of the service, the six of them filed onto the stage. Violet stood with Rose tucked against her side as Jessa stepped to the microphone.

"Thank you so much for coming today. Since Gran's death, we have been overwhelmed by the support and condolences offered. It seemed that our grandmother worked behind the scenes with people and helped many without any sort of recognition. I don't think we realized how much she was involved in the lives of people until this past week. She was a hard woman to get close to and even to live with sometimes. Like Dean said, she had some high expectations for those around her. But I loved her-" Jessa's voice cracked. She paused and cleared her throat before continuing. "I will miss her so very much. We wear white today at her request to celebrate her life rather than wear the dark colors to mourn her death. She will be missed. Our loss is heaven's gain."

Cami stood with her head bent the entire time Jessa spoke. Dean felt a little sorry for her, having to stand up in public just hours after the spectacle she'd made of herself. He would have loved to have been a fly on the wall once Jessa had found out what had happened. Whatever had been said, Cami was apparently toeing the line for the time being. Dressed much more modestly and conducting herself with reserve, it was hard to believe she was the same woman he'd handed off to Violet the night before.

The pastor closed the service with a prayer, and people began to move around. Some came to the front where the sisters were and talked with them, but most made their way to the exit. Dean noticed a tall, sandy-haired man standing behind Laurel and assumed it was her husband Matt. He'd heard Jessa and Julia both mention him, but this was the first time he'd seen him. Also standing with the group was Julia's lawyer, Stan Harrelson.

As Dean approached the group, Stan broke away and held out his hand. "Good to see you, Sheriff."

Dean shook hands with the older man. "You, too. Just wish it were under better circumstances."

"For Julia these are the best circumstances. She was ready to go," Stan said with a sad smile. "But I'll sure miss her. She kept me hopping."

"I can only imagine."

"Listen, I meant to call you last week but got caught up in a bunch of other stuff related to Julia's passing. There will be a reading of the will tomorrow afternoon at the manor. She requested that you be there."

"Is she expecting trouble or something?"

Stan laughed. "One might wonder, but no, she wants you there because you're mentioned in the will."

Dean straightened in surprise. "Me?"

"Yes. And I know you've had questions about why she did what she did for you. Tomorrow may help to answer those."

"Really?" Dean wondered if he really wanted to know now. Having already found out about one secret Julia had kept, he wasn't sure he was ready for any more big reveals.

"Really. The family is having the burial in the morning and then after lunch I'll read the will. It's happening so soon because there are some things that need to take place pretty quickly, plus Laurel needs to get back to her job. Not sure about Violet and Cami, but something tells me that for Cami, at least, getting out of this town can't happen soon enough."

"Okay. I'll be there," Dean assured him. The two of them approached the sisters who now stood with just the pastor and a few others near the stage.

"Hi, Dean," Violet said when she saw him. Up close he saw that in addition to the dress and heels, she wore makeup. Her brown eyes were friendly, though she looked tired. "Thank you for reading the Scripture and praying."

"It was my privilege." Dean smiled at her. "How are you doing?"

She tugged at her dress. "Ready to be out of this get-up and into something comfortable."

"You look very...beautiful."

Her eyes widened, and then she smiled, obviously pleased by his compliment. "Thank you. And you look very dashing in your uniform."

"I'd rather be in something more comfortable as well, but unfortunately, I'm required to wear this to earn a living."

"Are you on duty today?"

"No, not in the official sense, but I'm always on call, so to speak."

"I suppose that's true. Like last night."

"Yeah, like last night." Dean glanced to where Cami stood next to Lily and Rose. "How's she doing today?"

"Had a humdinger of a headache this morning. Jessa kept her mouth shut, but didn't bother to try and keep things quiet. I think she banged more pots and pans around than a galley full of chefs."

"Ouch," Dean said with a grin. "She looks like she's on her best behavior now."

"Oh, yes. Jessa might not have talked to her, but I said plenty this morning."

Dean saw Violet glance over at Cami. The younger woman tilted her head and, when Violet nodded, made her way over to them.

The two standing next to each other were like night and day. Like Jessa, Cami stood about three inches taller than Violet. Her blond hair hung to her shoulders in curls and though she wore expertly applied make-up, Dean could still see dark circles beneath her eyes.

"Sheriff," Cami said, holding out her hand. "I understand

I owe you an apology for last night, as well as thanks for rescuing me."

He shook her hand. "Just glad I was available to help out. You managed to scare my men into calling me."

She had the grace to look chagrined and glanced at Violet. "It won't happen again. Believe me."

"I'm glad to hear that. Things could have ended up much differently had the bartender not called the cops. Collingsworth is a nice little town, but there are men here who wouldn't hesitate to take advantage of a young woman like you."

Cami nodded. "I know."

"Well, apology accepted, and you're welcome."

She tipped her head to the side. "I didn't say anything too inappropriate, did I?"

Not wanting to add to the awkwardness of the situation, Dean said, "Let's just put this in the past and move on."

"Sounds good to me," Violet said. "Have you met Laurel and Matt?"

When he said he hadn't, Violet led him over to where they stood and introduced him. He noticed that Laurel didn't look very well, but wasn't sure if it was just the strain of the day or something more. She was pale, and her smile didn't reach her eyes. She was close to Violet in height, but her coloring was almost identical to Cami's. After chatting briefly he learned that Laurel was a home economics teacher at a high school in Minneapolis, and Matt worked in the construction industry.

"Looks like we need to clear out," the pastor said. "They want to close up."

Dean walked out to the parking lot with them. Violet thanked him again for his part in the service before heading to her car with Cami close behind. He was the last person to leave and turned his vehicle in the direction of the home where Addy was. Maybe, if she was up for it, they'd take a walk in the woods around their place. She wasn't a great outdoor kid. She took after her city girl mother in that regard, but sometimes she gave in and went with him on a short nature hike.

❧ Chapter Seven ❧

I said something embarrassing to him, didn't I?" Cami said as Violet drove through town. "He didn't say no when I asked him."

"He didn't say anything to me about it, but I'm sure you did. Your inhibitions were long gone by the time he got you out of there."

Cami sighed. "When is Jessa going to say something? I'm just waiting for the other shoe to drop."

"I don't know that she will." Violet glanced over to where Cami sat slumped in the passenger seat. "I told her I'd talk to you. She's got a lot on her plate right now. Just give her some space and don't do anything else stupid."

Cami didn't respond, so the rest of the trip to the manor was made in silence. Once Violet stopped the car, Cami got right out and headed inside. Violet moved a little more slowly. She was actually in no rush to go indoors. She missed being outside. It felt like it had been forever since she'd gone for a good long hike or bike ride. One more day and then she could escape for a bit. And follow up with Dean about finding her mother. She hadn't pressed the issue with so much else going on, but once they had their private funeral for Gran tomorrow and the reading of the will, she planned to ask him about it again.

As soon as she stepped into the house, Violet took off the heels that were killing her feet. Before doing anything else, she was going to get more comfortable. She could hear voices from the kitchen, but made her way upstairs to her room to change. Five minutes later, dressed in leggings and a sweatshirt and with her hair pulled back in a ponytail, Violet felt much more like herself.

In the kitchen, she found Jessa and Laurel with the younger girls. Cami was notably absent.

"Matt leave?" Violet asked as she slid onto one of the stools at the counter.

Laurel shook her head. "He's gone into town to pick up some food. Jessa phoned in an order for Chinese."

"Oh, yum. That sounds good."

When Matt came back with the food, Jessa sent Lily off to see if Cami wanted something to eat. Cami had changed as well when she joined them. With her hair pulled back and wearing an outfit similar to Violet's, she looked so young and innocent. Violet wished she could get into her sister's head sometimes, just to know what made her do the things she did.

As they ate the food Jessa had ordered, conversation flowed around everything but the subjects that were probably on everyone's mind. Gran's burial and the reading of the will the next day. Violet had no idea what could possibly be in the will. It was entirely possible Gran would leave everything to Jessa and the two younger girls since they were the ones who had been closest to her. Though she was fairly sure that there was a significant amount of money, Violet couldn't really venture a guess as to how much. Gran had deposited a thousand dollars into her bank account each month, and she figured the other girls got the same.

Violet didn't really care one way or the other about the money. Her freelance writing and photography were enough for her if she lived frugally. She wouldn't have minded a better car and a new mountain bike, but otherwise, money was not something she dwelled on a lot. By this time tomorrow it would all be over, and it would be time to figure out what to do next.

The sun shone brightly the next morning for the burial, but there was still a chill in the air. Violet found the burial to be unexpectedly difficult. The range of grief was palpable. From Jessa's sobs to Cami's stoic stubbornness, Violet found herself uncertain of how to react. They stood at the graveside, Gran's polished casket gleaming in the sunlight, a fractured family.

There had been a viewing of the body at the funeral home before coming to the cemetery. Violet hadn't been sure that Rose, or Lily for that matter, should have gone, but Jessa had insisted. Violet had stuck close to Rose when she realized that the girl's mother wasn't going to step up. She had balked at viewing the body, so Violet had moved her off to the side, glad that Jessa was too distracted by what was going on to object. She had been sure the girls would regret not seeing Gran one last time and saying goodbye.

Violet viewed the body, but didn't linger. The figure in the casket wasn't the woman she remembered. She would rather remember the energetic, vibrant woman her grandmother had been. It was a relief when they left the funeral home for the cemetery.

The pastor was there, along with his wife. The only other non-family member there was Stan. The service at the graveside was short and ended with each of them laying a rose from Jessa's greenhouse garden on the top of the casket. They probably could have stayed to watch the casket be lowered, but as soon as Lily and Rose laid their flowers, Cami began to move away from the graveside. Laurel and Matt followed, but Jessa lingered by the casket.

Rose tugged at her hand. Violet glanced down at the young girl.

"Can we go?" she whispered, an earnest look on her face.

Violet looked at Lily and saw the same look on the older girl's face. Knowing she risked the wrath of Jessa, Violet slid her arms around their shoulders and moved them slowly away from the graveside. Cami, Matt and Laurel all stood next to the limousine, but they didn't appear to be talking.

"Let's get the girls inside," Violet suggested as she approached. "It's a little chilly out here."

The driver had been sitting with his window open and got out at her words. He opened the door for them, and Violet ushered the girls in. Once they were in, Laurel and Cami followed.

"I'm going back to Jessa," Violet said when Matt motioned for her to precede him into the limo.

Wishing she'd worn shoes that made walking across the uneven ground to the graveside easier, Violet made her way back to Jessa. She slipped her arm around her waist and rested her head on Jessa's shoulder. Her older sister turned from the casket and wrapped her arms around Violet much like she had the day Violet had first arrived. Her own grief rose to meet Jessa's, as the pastor, his wife and Stan left them alone together.

It was a somber, silent ride back to the house once they joined the others in the limo. The pastor and his wife had come in their own car, as had Stan, so it was just the sisters and Matt, each caught up in their own world. The meal was equally subdued as they ate the lunch Miss Sylvia had come by the house to prepare for them.

Violet was relieved when Stan arrived for the reading of the will. As she sat on the loveseat in the library of the manor with Cami by her side, other people began to trickle in. Though Violet had expected that, there were a couple people present who surprised her. Dean, for one.

Stan stood at one end of the room, his briefcase open on the desk beside him. "Thank you all for coming. Each of you is here because Julia has left something for you in her will. I will begin by reading the parts that pertain to those of you who are non-family members. Once that is done, I will ask that you leave, as the remainder of the will is personal to the granddaughters and it will be up to them how much they make public."

Violet glanced at Jessa who was seated on a winged armchair across from her and lifted an eyebrow in question, but Jessa just shrugged.

Stan began to read all the legal parts of the beginning of the will, and then moved into the bequests. Violet wasn't surprised Gran had left something to each person who had worked at the manor with her. She left a few of them, like Miss Sylvia, some substantial amounts, and Violet knew it would change their lives. At the very end, Stan addressed Dean.

"To Dean Marconett, I leave the title to the home you are living in now as well as the cottage occupied by Sylvia Miller, with the understanding that she be allowed to continue to live there rent free as long as she should desire." In addition to the property, she also left him a large sum of money. Violet began to wonder if there really was a significant amount of money, or if there would be nothing left for them after all of this. "Dean, she also has a letter here for you. It will explain more about why she involved herself in your life the way she did. If you have any questions, give me a call."

Dean walked to where Stan stood to get the letter. "Thank you. I'm overwhelmed."

"It was important to Julia that she include you in this. I think you'll understand once you read the letter."

After Dean returned to his spot by the door, Stan thanked everyone for coming and dismissed those who had already been addressed, giving them instructions to get in contact with him in the next few days to begin the necessary steps to claim their bequests.

When it was just the sisters left in the room, Stan pulled a chair from behind the desk and sat down. He held the will in his hands and let his gaze go to each of them. "Julia wanted me to let each of you know that in spite of any differences she may have had with you, she loved you with all her heart. She wanted you to be happy in the life you've chosen, or in the case of the younger girls, may still choose. The Collingsworth name and legacy in this town were important to her, and she hopes that one or more of you will continue to carry that on."

He cleared his throat before continuing. "I know Julia was a private person, so you are probably unaware of the true value of her estate. She was a very wise woman when it came to money, and she worked hard over the years to invest the money and manage the property she inherited from her father. Her efforts paid off, and she has more than tripled the worth of the Collingsworth estate."

Violet swallowed hard, her stomach fluttering with nervousness.

"There are several different aspects to the estate. In addition to the money from some investments she had me liquidate a few months ago, there are also properties and other investments. And, of course, there is the manor. We will start with the money she has bequeathed to each of you." Stan looked down at the paper he held. "Any monies will be divided equally between all six girls with the funds for the underage ones to be held in trust until they are of legal age. Currently her account, after the amounts already bequeathed are removed, sits at thirty million dollars."

Violet wasn't the only one who gasped at the amount. Never had she thought it would be so substantial. This was life changing. She glanced at Cami and saw the shock on her face as well.

Stan looked around the room and then continued, "Properties will be held jointly by all six. Any money made from the properties will be divided evenly. Decisions to sell any of the properties listed below must be agreed on by each person. Finally, the manor. It is to be held jointly by all of you. However, all of this is dependent on one thing."

A catch. Violet almost smiled. It didn't surprise her at all that Gran had attached strings to the money she'd worked so hard to earn. In fact, Violet would have been a bit disappointed if the woman hadn't. This was so very much like her.

"What do we have to do?" Cami asked.

"In order to claim all aspects of your inheritance, the six of you must stay here for a month and help renovate it."

"Stay for a month?" Laurel asked.

"Renovate it?" Jessa said at the same time.

"Yes. Julia realized that due to jobs and such, the month can't happen right away, but sometime in the next year, you girls need to decide on a month when you can all be here. Everything for the renovation has already been arranged."

"What do you mean?" Jessa asked.

"Your grandmother has already picked the person to do the renovations. She has worked with him to design the plans and all the money has been set aside to pay for the work. It was her desire to bring the manor up to date, yet still keep the vision her father had for it. And should you girls all agree, she was hoping you'd maybe consider opening it as a bed and breakfast."

"That surprises me," Jessa said. "I often talked to her about that, but she was always opposed."

"I think it was something she opposed while she lived here. I think this was her way of giving permission if that was what you still wanted to do it. That is not a requirement in the way the month long stay here during the renovation is."

"Why would she require that?" Cami asked.

"She wanted you girls to spend time here, working together, in hopes that it would bring you closer to each other. You're what is left of the Collingsworth family."

"And if only some of us agree to do the month? Do we all lose our inheritance?" Laurel asked Stan.

"She has made provisions for that scenario, but she preferred to give you the chance to work it out together."

Violet wondered how difficult this was going to be. Jessa and Cami seemed to disagree on things on principle alone. She really hoped they wouldn't make this too difficult. "How soon do we have to let you know?"

"Obviously the sooner you decide and complete the month, the sooner you'll have the money. The monthly amounts she's been giving to each of you will continue until the final pay out of the inheritance."

When no one said anything more, Stan tied it up by encouraging them to call him if they had any questions at all. Jessa walked him to the front door, while the others sat in stunned silence. Violet hoped they could decide on a time sooner rather than later, not because she wanted the money, but because she didn't want to have to put her life on hold indefinitely.

✌ *Chapter Eight* ✍

WHEN Jessa came back, she stood in the middle of the room. "Okay. Obviously this is a lot to take in. I never had a clue that she'd do something like this, but it's important that we try to work with her stipulations. Anyone care to toss out a suggestion for a month? Keeping in mind jobs and such. I'm fairly flexible since I live here, so I'll let others make suggestions first."

"I would prefer sooner rather than later," Violet said. "I don't want to get caught up in another work project only to have to drop it to come home again."

"Same here," said Cami.

"I guess I'm the one that will hold things up," Laurel said. "Obviously I can't get out of school for a month. We'll have to wait until school is over."

"That's not too far away," Jessa commented. "When is school done for the year?"

"I'm not sure of the exact date, but it's usually the first week of June."

"So I'm guessing it doesn't have to be an exact month, but thirty days. We could clarify that with Stan, but if that's the case, maybe our month could start June fifteenth," Jessa suggested.

That would mean a two month wait. Violet figured she could live with that. It would give her a chance to hang around town and continue her search for their mother. "I'm good with that. I'll probably just stay here until then, if that's okay, Jess."

"That would be fine," Jessa assured her. "Cami?"

Cami bit her lip. "Yes, I guess that would work for me too. I will have to go away for a bit, but I'll be back by then."

Jessa looked around in surprise. "Did we just agree? In less than ten minutes?"

"It's a minor miracle," Violet agreed with a laugh.

"I'll let Stan know what we've decided," Jessa said. "And then...well, life goes on."

Violet didn't move after Jessa had left the room. "Where on earth did Gran get so much money?"

"Yeah, no kidding," Cami murmured. "Never would have guessed she had that much sitting around."

"Actually," Laurel began, "I did a little research a few years back."

Violet looked to where Laurel sat with Matt. "Really? Why?"

Laure shrugged. "No real specific reason. I guess I just wanted to know more about the Collingsworth family and why it was so important to Gran. She was a little nuts about the legacy of it."

"This is true," Violet agreed. None of them had had fathers listed on their birth certificates, so they all had the Collingsworth last name. Gran had constantly reminded them of the legacy of the name they bore. There were plenty of times Violet had wished she could divest herself of the name. "What did you find out?"

"At the turn of the century, the Collingsworths were already rich. They had come from England in the late 1800's, and immediately began to build their fortune. Not one to parade wealth in front of others, William Collingsworth invested in gold and properties first in New York, then Chicago and finally Minneapolis. An astute businessman, he was extremely cautious with his money. He didn't take big risks, but those he did take paid off for him a little at a time. This." Laurel waved her hand in the air. "Was his one big expenditure. Apparently he wanted the seclusion of living away from the big city, but still being close for business purposes. He wanted to have plenty of room for his family and any guests they had.

"He had just finished building it when the depression hit. But because he had not invested in the stock market or trusted the banks with his money, the Collingsworths came through it relatively unscathed. During that time, William was able to pick up depressed stocks for things like oil, and also he bought more properties. After the depression ended, the stocks and property values began to rise and his wealth shot through the roof. Apparently he wasn't one to trust something that had already failed so alarmingly, but he waited until the values of his stocks were quite high and then began to slowly sell them off."

"So how much was the family worth at that point?" Violet asked.

Laurel shook her head. "There were no figures I could find that would pinpoint exactly how rich William was. He was an intensely private person who had a passion for God and living a relatively simple life. Many shared after his death how he helped them, so it appears that while he was rich, he wasn't stingy. His son—Gran's father—learned well from his father and also increased the wealth of the family. By then the town of Collingsworth had sprung up due to the college being established. We all know the history of that and how that was something William had asked his son to do. Then Gran just carried on after her father."

"Well, that certainly gives a bit more perspective, but still...thirty million plus properties? Crazy." But having heard the history of the money, Violet felt the weight of not squandering this financial blessing. She would have to spend some time thinking and researching to see how she, too, could grow the gift God had given their family and yet still share it with others.

"You ready to go?" Matt asked Laurel.

"Heading back to the city?" Violet had thought they might stay the night, but knew they both had jobs to get back to.

"Yes, I think most everything is tied up here, and we need to get back for work," Laurel said.

"I think I'm going to head back as well," Cami piped in. "I have some things I need to take care of before I can come back for the month."

And with that, the family reunion was over. It didn't take long for Cami to pack or Matt and Laurel to gather up their things. Soon Jessa, Violet and the younger girls were standing on the front steps waving goodbye as the two cars pulled out of the driveway.

Jessa let out a long sigh. "At least we're all still alive."

"But we still got that month ahead," Violet commented. "That will be the true test."

"I don't even want to think about that." Jessa turned to go back into the house.

Violet draped an arm over Rose's shoulders and followed Lily inside. "What are you girls going to do now?"

"Jessa said I could help her in the greenhouse," Rose said.

"I've got a project to work on for school that's due tomorrow," Lily said with a frown. "I have to finish it up."

"Well, I think I'm going to go for a hike if no one needs me," Violet informed them.

Jessa smiled. "I'm surprised you've lasted this long without your outdoor ventures."

Violet nodded. "I'm in need of some alone time with nature. I'll be back before supper."

"Have fun," Jessa said as she grabbed Rose's hand. "Take your phone though, in case we need to get hold of you."

Ten minutes later, dressed in a pair of old fitted jeans,

sturdy hiking boots and a hoodie, Violet stepped out of the house into the sunshine. She took a deep breath of the fresh air and then headed for a trail she'd hiked on many years ago. It was somewhat overgrown, but she was able to find where it started and go from there. The trees had thickened over the past few years, but soon her path took her close to the lake's edge. She decided she'd hike to the north point of the lake, spend a bit of time there and then head back. There was a clearing with a large rock along the shore where she'd spent a lot of time as a teenager.

With only nature for company, Violet's energy began to renew itself. She felt more calm and at peace than she had since she'd arrived. This was definitely something she needed. It was a good time to take a break between the funeral and the next difficult thing she needed tackle. Finding out what she could about their mom. But for now, it was her, God and nature. and that was more than enough.

⁓∞⁓

Dean had hiked around the northern point of the lake and then headed back. He'd been gone longer than normal, but after the reading of the will, he'd needed some space to think. Fortunately Sylvia had agreed to watch Addy if she got home before he did. As the trees thinned near the lake's shore, Dean found an opening and stepped out onto the rocky beach. He walked for a bit before he found a flat rock that he could sit on.

The letter Stan had handed him had definitely answered his questions, and it had also cast Julia Collingsworth in a new light. He never would have guessed at the sentimentality she'd shared in the letter she'd written to him in the weeks before her death. And having her leave him the property and money had shocked him.

The sound of someone or something moving through the trees drew Dean's attention. He looked to see if he could spot what made the noise. There was wildlife in the area, and he'd run across deer a few times, but this didn't sound like deer. Suddenly a figure appeared, head bent as they walked along the rocks in his direction.

As the person drew closer, Dean recognized who it was and smiled. Not wanting to frighten her, but needing to alert her to his presence, he said, "Hey!"

Violet's head jerked up as she came to an abrupt stop. The surprise on her face melted into a smile. "Hey. I didn't expect to see you...or anyone, for that matter, out here." She came to stand next to the rock where he sat.

"I needed some time to think. Hiking in these woods is usually my retreat from the world." He motioned to the rock next to him. "Wanna sit?"

Violet nodded. She pulled a water bottle from the pocket of her hoodie and took a drink. "Yeah, I'm not used to being inside so much. I needed a break."

"I hear ya." Dean stared out across the water. "So, the will reading was a bit of a surprise. I didn't expect your grandmother to leave me anything."

"She left you a letter too, right?"

"Yeah." Dean touched the pocket of his jacket where he'd put it earlier. "I'd always wondered why she had helped me out, and now I know."

"Want to share?" Violet asked.

❧ *Chapter Nine* ❧

DEAN glanced at her. "Well, the short story is that I am the grandson of the man your grandmother loved and wanted to marry. Unfortunately, he was the son of the gardener and housekeeper, and her father wanted her to do better. She said that her grandfather tried to convince her father otherwise, but in the end, my grandfather's family moved away, and Julia went on to marry a more appropriate man. Did you ever know your grandfather?"

Violet shook her head. "He was dead by the time I came to live with Gran. I always wondered about him though. Given that Gran was an only child and a girl, the Collingsworth name would have ended with her, but I guess they somehow convinced my grandfather to take her last name instead of her taking his. Gran never really talked much about him or how that whole issue was dealt with."

"Well, I guess at some point after his death, she had her lawyer track down her old love. By that point he was married and had kids and grandkids of his own. By all accounts he was happy, so she left well enough alone. However, Julia being Julia, she kept tabs on us, and when I needed some help a few years back, she stepped in."

"Wow. So your grandfather was like her one true love?"

"I guess so. From the letter, it sounded like she was heartbroken when he left. She said your grandfather was a good man, and in time she came to love him, but never like she had loved my grandpa."

"I have a hard time picturing Gran harboring such love and heartache. She hid it well."

"Yes, it surprised me." Dean paused. "Actually, I was kind of concerned when Stan said he had a letter that explained everything. After talking with you about Rose, I realized that Julia Collingsworth might be a woman with more than one secret."

"What did you think the letter would say?" Violet asked, her expression curious.

"I was kind of afraid it was going to say that I was her grandson or something like that."

Violet laughed. "Yeah, I suppose anything is a possibility when it comes to Gran, but I think you're a little old to be a child of my mom's. And she was an only child. Why did that idea make you afraid though? We're not that bad a family."

Dean shook his head. "No, you're not. It's just..." He let his voice trail off, knowing he was a little too close to revealing something he wasn't completely sure about just yet. "Well, I wouldn't have known how to deal with finding out my family wasn't really my family. Definitely would have been disconcerting."

"Yeah. No doubt about that." She bit her lower lip. "I wonder sometimes if we're right in not revealing the truth about Rose now. But that's not my call, so I have to go with what the others think."

Dean looked at her. She gazed at him with emotion in her brown eyes. The sun made her dark hair shine, showing off bits of auburn in its strands. His breath caught in his lungs.

Looking away, he said, "Secrets can be damaging even when kept for the best reasons."

"Yes. I may try and press my point again, but last time I

brought it up, it was not well received."

"I'm sure it's not an easy decision. Maybe given a little time, it might be easier to make. Especially since Julia's gone now." He glanced at her and saw her nod. "Are you going to be heading back home now that it's all over?"

"Not right away. Besides, home is kinda anywhere I hang my hat. For the moment, my hat is hung here."

"You don't have a place or job to get back to?"

"Nope. I brought pretty much all my stuff with me. Only things I left behind were my mountain bike and skis. I figured if I don't end up going back to Seattle I'll have them shipped to wherever I am."

Her comments were a pointed reminder of how different her lifestyle was from his. "So you've never really put down roots after leaving here?"

Violet shook her head. "No, not really. I go where my job and fancy take me. I've slept in my car a few times, but usually have a friend or two I can bunk with for a while. This last stretch has been the longest I've been in one place."

"How long was that?"

"I've been staying with a friend in Seattle for the past nine months. She let me use the extra room in her apartment, but she was getting married, so I had to be out by the end of the month. I hadn't found any other place yet, though I had a couple of leads. When the call came about Gran, I just packed up the car and left."

"So you might not go back?" Dean wanted to punch himself for sounding so hopeful, and he hoped Violet didn't pick up on it.

She shrugged. "I'm not sure. I'll go back for the wedding, but I was already thinking of moving on from Seattle. Just hadn't settled on where I'd go next."

"You're quite different from Jessa. She told me once that she had never even left the state."

Violet smiled. "Yes, Jessa is definitely a homebody. So is Laurel, actually. She didn't go too far. Just far enough to get out from under Gran, but still close enough to be in familiar country. Cami and I, we're the wanderers in the family."

Dean hated the jumble of emotions that were tangled up inside him with her revelations. "So you don't see yourself settling down and having a family?"

Violet met his gaze, her expression guarded. "To be honest, I don't usually look too far into the future. One day at a time is how I usually take things. And trusting God to lead me to the right place at the right time. I would imagine God will either do one of two things when...if...I find the right man. He will make him a man with a wandering spirit like mine, or He'll give me the desire to stay put and finally call one place home."

"But that hasn't happened yet?" Dean could see the wariness on Violet's face and realized he'd better back off. "Sorry. It's the cop in me." He smiled, hoping to make her relax. "You're just so different from Jessa and Julia. I'm curious how that is."

Violet returned his smile, her expression relaxing. "Yes, I am very different from them both. Thankfully, Gran eventually realized when I graduated that she couldn't contain me and let me go with her...reluctant blessing and after some heated arguments."

"I'm sure she would have loved to see all of you settled and happy before she died."

Violet nodded. "No doubt, but you just can't force love. Plus, I don't think any of us realized how sick she really was. Certainly it came as a surprise to me. Just another one of the secrets she kept close to her heart."

"You seem to be handling your grief fairly well. How are the others?"

Violet stared out at the water. Her profile showed the gentle slope of her nose and full lips. She blinked rapidly a couple of times. "I think I did my grieving on my trip here from Seattle." She glanced at him. "Not that I should mention this to a cop, but I did my share of crying as I drove. And praying. With my eyes open."

Dean held his hands up. "I'm off duty."

Violet smiled. "I had a few conversations with Gran too." She touched her chest. "I'm at peace, and I know that she is too. But the others? Especially Cami. I really don't know."

"I remember how it was when my grandpa died. It did take some time to sink in. He was an important part of my life, and it took a while before I stopped picking up the phone to call him. Or thinking about how much he'd like to know about something that had happened in my life. I still have that odd moment, but it's now happy memories and not so much sadness."

"Death is always hard. I fear that Cami will have the most trouble with Gran's death, though I may be wrong."

"Because she butted heads with Julia so much?" Dean asked.

"Yeah. I really think we all figured Gran would live forever. Like death wouldn't dare take her before she was ready to go."

"But maybe she *was* ready to go," Dean said softly. He expected Violet to object, but instead she looked at him, her eyes looking more like liquid chocolate.

"Yes. I'm beginning to think she was. She had a lot of heartache. More than we realized apparently given what she told you in the letter. I think maybe she was ready to leave it all behind her."

As they sat in silence, Dean wished he could offer her comfort, but knew that was not his place. Still, his heart ached for her. For the first time in such a very long time, a woman was making her way past the defenses he kept in place. And by all appearances, she wasn't even trying to breach those walls. His stomach clenched at the thought that he was being drawn to a woman who wasn't interested in him.

Please, God, don't let that be the case.

She pulled her phone out of her pocket and checked it. "I need to head back. I told Jess I'd be back for supper. It takes me about forty-five minutes to hike to the manor from here."

As they slid off the rock, Dean said, "I'd offer to walk you home, but since that's pretty much the opposite direction, and I need to get back home as well, I'm not going to be able to."

"That's fine. Just gives me a little more time to think."

"I'll give you a call later with the information for the guy I told you about." Dean said.

Violet's expression brightened. "The one to help me find my mom?"

Dean nodded.

"That would be great. I'm excited to get some help with that."

As he watched her walk away, he wished he'd been a little more obvious in how he was feeling. But there was a voice in his head that said, *"Too soon!"*

Well, it wasn't like he'd wanted to ask her to marry him, just to consider getting to know each other better. She intrigued him. Had from the moment he'd walked up to her car window and looked down into a pair of warm brown eyes.

She doesn't seem to like to put down roots.

Dean couldn't argue with that. Both Jessa and Julie had mentioned how she liked to move around, that roaming was in her blood, and she'd confirmed that. She was definitely the opposite from him in that regard. He couldn't be more firmly rooted than he was in his job and life in Collingsworth. But she'd mentioned being willing to settle down for the right man. Was it a foolish desire to hope that might be him?

You haven't told her about Addy. Maybe she doesn't want a ready-made family. Or kids at all.

If any of the arguments held weight, that one did. He didn't really want to introduce the two of them until he was sure Violet was even interested in him. Addy was at that point where she talked about wanting a mom. Introducing Violet to her would no doubt increase that desire in the little girl. And if Violet was iffy on settling down with a man, she might be even less willing to consider a man with a child. But maybe if she gave seemed to return his feelings and was willing to give them a chance as a couple, then Addy's presence in his life wouldn't be as daunting.

Dean turned toward the path he'd taken earlier that had brought him to the lake shore and the surprising meeting with Violet. It took him away from the woman who occupied his thoughts so much these days, but gave him plenty of time to think on his way home.

જ્જ

Violet stumbled over a root, grabbing onto a tree to keep from falling. The conversation with Dean played over and over in her head, distracting her from the path. She stood for a moment, hand braced against the rough bark of the tree, listening to the sounds of the forest and seeking some peace from it.

The last thing she'd ever thought would happen when she returned to Collingsworth would be meeting a man who intrigued her in a way that no man had. She had met lots of men in her travels, was good friends with many of them and had even dated a few. But none had stopped her in her tracks and made her look twice like Dean Marconett had. In the short time they'd known each other she'd seen several different sides to the man. The business side of him when he'd pulled her over. The gentlemanly side of him when he'd stopped by with the information for her car. Then the night he'd brought Cami home she'd seen his caring and protective nature. And finally at the funeral she'd seen the spiritual man he was as he'd read the Scripture and prayed.

If she ever had listed the things she wanted in a man, Dean would probably have fulfilled most. But was she ready to even consider a relationship that might very well tie her to a place she couldn't wait to escape from ten years earlier? Things were a little different now with her grandmother's domineering presence gone. But soon she would have the money to travel all she wanted and could settle some place far, far away from Collingsworth. But was that the right thing to do?

She sensed that perhaps Dean was interested in her too, given the questions he'd been asking earlier. And she hadn't missed the pleased look on his face when she'd come across him on the rock. The thought warmed her in a way no other man's interest had. And there had been many men interested in her over the years. A couple of those guys had been so nice that she'd wished she'd felt something for them, but there had been nothing but friendship there. This was different and new. And confusing.

She pushed away from the tree. Keeping her head down and gaze focused on the path, Violet realized she hadn't prayed much about her future in the past few years. She'd just drifted along, grateful for jobs that came her way which allowed her to use her gifts. However she was staring thirty in the face. Maybe it was time to consider settling down somewhere. But was that somewhere Collingsworth? And with someone like Dean? Never mind someone *like* Dean. *With* Dean?

Her mind worked through all the pros and cons as she made her way back to the manor. She was glad Dean hadn't been upfront about what he was feeling...if he was feeling like she was. It gave her a little bit of breathing space. Maybe a call to her friend in Seattle was in order. She wished she could talk to her sister, but she was pretty sure Jessa would have an opinion on things. Right now she needed to be able to trust her own heart and judgment maybe with a little guidance from a friend who had gone down this path.

It was quiet in the house with the others gone, so after supper Violet retreated to her room and worked on the article she was doing for a travel magazine and edited the pictures that were to go with it. The work was a welcome distraction as she waited to see if Dean would call like he'd said.

It was just before ten when her cell phone chirped. His name popped up on the display since she'd added his name to her contact list. She took a deep breath before tapping the screen to answer.

❧ *Chapter Ten* ❧

"Good evening," he replied when she answered. "How has the rest of your day gone?"

Violet settled back against the headboard of her bed, her feet flat on the mattress. She told him about the sisters leaving and how it had been nice to have a bit of peace and quiet with just Jessa and the youngest two.

"Did the rest of will reading contain any more surprises? I forgot to ask earlier at the lake."

"Oh. Well, nothing like revealing any more siblings or where my mom is, but Gran is making us work for our inheritance. Which was something of a surprise."

"The inheritance or that she's making you work for it?" Dean asked.

Violet laughed. "Definitely not that she's making us work for it. That has Gran written all over it. The shock came in the size of her estate, and the amounts that are being left to each of us."

"I was very surprised with what she left to me. I never in a million years had expected that. When Stan first told me I needed to be at the reading of the will, I figured he was expecting trouble and needed law enforcement on hand." Dean laughed, and the deep warmth of it sent tingles down Violet's spine. "I am very grateful for her generosity."

"It sounds like she has a soft spot for you because of your grandfather. She probably figures you could have been her grandson. And with the lot she ended up with as granddaughters, you would have been her favorite, no doubt."

"Well, like I said earlier, I'm glad that wasn't her revelation. For a lot of reasons."

Violet twisted a piece of hair around her finger. "Yes, I'm glad for your sake too."

There was a beat of silence before Dean cleared his throat and said, "Um, about this search for your mother. Now more than I ever I feel obliged to keep my promise to Julia. I hope you understand that."

"I do completely. And I have to say I...admire that about you. She wouldn't know the difference now, but you still are a man of your word."

"That being said, I have spoken with someone who can help you. I will text you his number. He's expecting your call. And that's as far as I'll be able to go with this. I'm sorry."

"Don't apologize! I understand completely," Violet told him. "Are you interested in hearing progress reports? I would love to keep you in the loop, if you don't feel that it would compromise your promise to Gran."

"Sure, I would like to know how the search is going. I do hope you're able to find what you're looking for even though Julia seemed to want to keep you in the dark about it all."

"Since I was the one who knew her the best, even if I was only six years old when she dropped me off, I figure it's my responsibility to find her or find out what happened to her."

"Yeah, I understand that. I just hope it's a positive outcome."

"Me too, but I've prepared myself...I think...for the worst."

"So changing the subject a bit," Dean said. "I was curious about your job. The one that allows you to travel so much. What exactly is it that you do? If you don't mind telling me, that is."

Violet hesitated, a bit surprised at the personal turn of their conversation. But she would answer his questions, because if there was something sparking between them, she wanted all the cards on the table so he could know how she lived her life. "I don't mind. I'm a freelance writer and photographer for a few travel magazines and blogs, so I travel for that. I'm very much an outdoors person, so I enjoy traveling and experiencing different environments. I've done pretty much every outdoor activity there is, but hiking is probably still my favorite thing to do, as it allows me to move at a slower pace and actually enjoy nature."

"I always have enjoyed being outside, but it wasn't until I moved here that I really started to get into things like hiking and skiing."

"That path I took to the shore today was one I used a lot as a teenager. No one else in the family enjoyed being outside like I did, so I was pretty much guaranteed my privacy. No nagging, no fighting. Just me and nature."

"Was that why you were out there today?" Dean asked.

"Well, by the time I set out, any fighting was pretty much done since Laurel and Cami had left. I just needed time to refresh and rejuvenate myself."

"You're not one of those people who are energized by being around other people?"

Violet laughed. "No, not at all. It's okay if it's just one or two people who are placing demands on me, but these past few days..."

"I can only imagine," Dean said. "When will you be all together again?"

"Oh. Yeah. I didn't tell you yet, did I? Gran's will said that the only way we'll get our inheritance is if we all come back to the manor for a month to help renovate it. So we had to decide on a month when we could all be here to fulfill the terms of her will."

"Really?" Violet heard a note of excitement in Dean's voice.

"Yeah. There was no way we could do it right away since Laurel is still teaching. She couldn't come until she was done."

"So when did you decide on?"

"We're checking with Stan to see if it has to be a calendar month or if it can just be thirty days. If it can be thirty days, the plan is for us to all be back here on June fifteenth."

"That's over two months away. Are you going to stick around Collingsworth?"

Violet bit her lip. "For the most part. I have an article due that will require me to travel to Colorado for a couple of days, and then I need to go back to Seattle for my friend's wedding, but aside from that, I'll probably be here."

"I'm glad to hear that." There was a pause then Dean cleared his throat and said, "I'm sure Jessa will be glad of your company. And uh, Lily and Rose too."

Violet warmed at his words. "Yes, I think I owe it to Jessa to stay and help for a bit. As long as she needs me."

They talked for a little longer before Dean said, "I guess I'd better go. Have to be at work early tomorrow. I'll text you that number before I go to bed though."

"Thank you. I will call him tomorrow and let you know how it goes."

As she disconnected the call, Violet found herself smiling. The call with Dean had been more comfortable than she'd thought it might be. She liked that they could converse easily. It was just one more thing she liked about him. One more thing that warmed her heart. One more thing that prodded her down that new and strange road toward the unknown. And for the first time in her life, the unknown scared her.

Jessa headed into town to her shop the next morning

while the girls went to school. Alone in the house, Violet called the number Dean had given her the previous evening. After five rings, she was just about to hang up when the call was answered.

"Hello?"

"Hi. Is this Tom Davis?"

"Yep. That's me."

"Um...Dean Marconett gave me your number. He said you might be able to help me find out what happened to my mother."

"Ah, yes. You must be Violet Collingsworth."

"Yes. Sorry. Should have mentioned that." Violet tried to ignore the butterflies that flitted in her stomach. This was the first time she felt that there was a decent chance of finding her mom.

"No worries." She heard noise like paper rustling in the background. "Do you have pen and paper?"

"No, but I do have my laptop which is where I usually take notes."

"That's fine. Here's my email address." He repeated it twice to make sure she had it correct. "Now, I'm going to need some information. If you could compile everything you know about your mother and email it to me, I'll have a good place to start."

"How far back?"

"No detail is too small. Birthdate, for sure. If you could get me a copy of her birth certificate, that would be helpful. Also her social security number. And then dates and locations where you know she lived. And detail the information of the last time you had contact with her. I'll read through it and give you call back if I have questions."

"Thank you. I appreciate you being willing to take this on."

"Not a problem, little lady. I love a good challenge." Tom chuckled. "Didn't Dean warn you about me?"

"Uh...no, he just said you'd be the best person to help me."

"Ha! Guess he's learned to respect his elders. We were partnered together when he was a rookie cop. It took a while, but I got that boy to toe the line and turned him into a top notch detective. Good enough to be Sheriff."

"You've known him for a long time then?"

"Yep. I retired from the force a few years back, but can't seem to give up the detecting side of things. I will do my best to find your mama. I make no promises on a happy reunion, but you will hopefully have some sort of resolution."

"That's what I want," Violet assured him. "I'll have this information to you sometime today."

"Excellent! I'm ready for something to sink my teeth into."

His excitement rubbed off on Violet, and she hung up the phone filled with hope and eager to compile the information he had asked for. Time passed quickly as she worked, and, before she knew it, Jessa was home for lunch.

"What are you typing so madly about?" Jessa asked as she opened the fridge.

Violet saved her file and closed the lid of the laptop. "It's a project that I'm working on."

She didn't want to lie to Jessa, but of all the sisters, she was the one who had the least interest in their mother. Telling her what she was doing would most likely lead to an argument. And it might all be for naught if Tom Davis couldn't find anything on their mother. If he did...well, she'd cross that bridge when she got to it.

"Want a sandwich?" Jessa asked as she placed some deli meat and bread on the counter.

"Sure." Violet stood to help her get their lunch ready. "How was the shop?"

"It's fine. I never have a worry when Daphne's in charge. She loves the shop like it's her own, so it runs smoothly when I'm not in." Jessa's small shop featured the fresh vegetables and flowers she grew in the large greenhouse behind the manor. Violet doubted it was the most profitable business around given the cost of keeping the greenhouse functioning during the cold winters, but Jessa loved growing things.

One good thing about all of them was that they had been able to move into areas they loved. Combining her love for the outdoors and travel with writing and photography fulfilled Violet. She knew the greenhouse was a joy for Jessa, and Laurel's passion for homemaking had been a good fit for the job she held now teaching home economics to high school students. And while she knew Cami was involved in the music business in some way, Violet wasn't completely sure what she did. Periodically she would search her out on the internet but could never find anything about her in the music industry. She knew that Cami longed for fame and fortune as a singer, much like their mother had, but it had not come her way just yet. Of all of them, the inheritance money would probably be most welcome by Cami. Somehow Violet knew that whatever gigs she got, weren't making her younger sister rich or famous.

"Are you going back to the shop this afternoon?" Violet asked as they ate their lunch together.

Jessa shook her head. "I'm going to work some in the greenhouse. You hanging around here?"

"Yep. Have to get this preliminary information submitted today, so I need to finish that up."

After cleaning up, Jessa disappeared out the back door. Violet thought about moving her stuff upstairs, but decided to just stay at the table until she was finished. A couple of hours later she was reading over all the information she'd compiled when the phone rang.

Her heart skipped a beat when she saw Dean's name on the display. With a smile, she answered the call.

"How are you doing?" Dean asked when she answered.

"Pretty good. How about you?"

"It's been a pretty quiet day, so I can't complain. Did you get hold of Tom Davis?"

"Yes! He was an interesting guy to talk to. Hang on. I'm just going to move upstairs so I'm not overheard," Violet said, glancing toward the back door. Tucking the phone between her shoulder and ear, she began to gather up her stuff. She didn't want Jessa to walk in on her talking about their mother. Once upstairs, she settled on the window seat that looked out over the wooded area that stood between the manor and the lake. "I didn't realize you'd worked with him. I thought he was just someone you knew from being a cop."

"Tom's an old and dear friend. He got me through some rough times and taught me everything I know about being a good cop."

"He spoke highly of you, too. And he seemed excited to get to work on finding my mom."

"When I told him about it, he was very intrigued. If anyone can find her or information on her, it will be Tom."

"Now it will just be a test of my patience," Violet said with a laugh. "It's going to take a lot of restraint to keep from calling him every day to ask what's up."

"I'm sure Tom realizes how important this is to you. He'll give you a call as soon as he has anything."

"My phone will never leave my side." Violet heard voices in the hallway and glanced over in time to see Rose peek her head into the room. "Looks like the girls are home from school. Guess I'd better go see how their day went. Thanks again for pointing me in Tom Davis's direction."

"And again, you're welcome. Have a good evening."

Violet said goodbye and then stood, tucking the phone into her pocket as she walked to the doorway. "Hey, sweetie." Rose skipped into the room and gave Violet a hug. "How was your day?"

"Good! I don't even have homework tonight."

"Well, that's always a good thing." Keeping an arm around the girl's shoulders, Violet walked down the stairs with her to the kitchen.

Jessa and Lily appeared to be in the middle of a

discussion about a boy. And from the sound of it, Jessa wasn't too happy about whoever it was.

Rose tugged her hand. Violet bent down so the girl could whisper in her ear. "Nate Proctor asked Lily out on a date."

"Is he nice?" Violet asked.

"Yes. And Lily thinks he's cute too."

"He's too old for her," Jessa said abruptly.

Violet looked at Lily. The teenager stood with her arms crossed, biting her lower lip. "How old is he?"

Lily glanced at Jessa and then back to Violet. "He's twenty."

"He's too old," Jessa repeated. "She's only seventeen years old."

Violet sighed. It appeared the drama hadn't left with Cami after all. "Is that your only objection to him, Jess?"

"What do you mean?" Jessa also stood with crossed arms, but her expression was set, not uncertain like Lily's.

"I mean, do you have other objections to him? Is he a bad influence? A drug dealer?"

"Well, no. He's a decent guy. He works at his father's garage. They go to our church."

Violet turned to her teenage sister. "Lily, you're going to be eighteen in three months. I think if this Nate guy is really serious about you, he'll be willing to wait. If he respects you, he'll respect Jessa's wishes. And if not, it's better you find that out now."

Lily's head dipped. "Is it okay if we do stuff together with a group? Like going bowling with the young adults?"

Violet glanced at Jessa, hoping she'd be willing to compromise a bit too. She read the war on Jessa's face. Violet knew she didn't want to give an inch, but in the end, Jessa nodded. "That would be okay, but you both have to understand there will be no dating with just the two of you until you're eighteen and out of school."

Lily lifted her head, a small smile on her face. She went

and hugged Jessa. "Thanks, Jessa. I promise we'll do as you ask."

Jessa rested her cheek on the top of Lily's head. Violet knew she felt the weight of the responsibility of the two young girls now that Gran had passed. "I love you, Lily Belle. Just want you to be safe. And happy."

That issue behind them, Violet was able to enjoy the rest of the evening with her sisters. They spent some time after supper in the greenhouse with Jessa. While Violet did prefer the real outdoors, she had to admire the set-up Jessa had.

As she lay in bed later that night with her curtains open so she could see the stars in the dark sky, Violet again let her thoughts go to the possibility of settling down in Collingsworth. It was sad and maybe wrong, but the thought was a little more appealing now that Gran wasn't there to dictate her life. Violet punched her pillow and curled on her side. She hated that she had had a better long distance relationship with Gran than when she'd lived at the manor. But the less Gran had known about her life, the better the relationship they'd had. Coming back to stay while Gran was still alive had never been an option. But now...

⁂ Chapter Eleven ⁂

THE next morning Violet took the girls into town for school and then drove to the mechanic's to drop off her car. As she pulled into the parking lot, the name on the sign registered. *Proctor Repairs*. Curious to see if she'd run into Nate, Violet walked into the office.

There was a young man standing at a slightly beat up counter working on a computer. He looked up as she walked in and smiled. "Hello. How can I help you?"

"I had an appointment to drop my car off today to have the speedometer fixed." Violet looked at the name on his blue coveralls. *Nate. Bingo*. "You're Nate Proctor?"

The young man's eyebrows raised a fraction. "Yes, I am."

Violet held out her hand. "Nice to meet you. I'm Violet Collingsworth, Lily's sister."

Recognition dawned on his face. He took her hand and gave it a firm shake. "Nice to meet you. Lily said her sisters were all in town."

"I'm the only out-of-town one still hanging around, I'm afraid."

"Well, we'll take really good care of your car. One of us will give you a call when we have an idea of what's wrong and how much it will cost." Nate took the keys she held out and then clicked the mouse a couple of times, looking at the computer screen. "It looks like Dad already put your information into the system when you called for the appointment."

Violet thanked him and then left the garage. She could have walked back to the manor. It wouldn't have been the first time she'd walked the couple of miles from town, but she decided to go get some breakfast and write a few emails instead.

She crossed Main Street and walked a couple blocks to the cafe. The sound of people talking, the clatter of dishes and the warm aroma of fried foods and coffee greeted Violet as she opened the door and stepped inside. It was like being pulled back in time a decade. Not much, if anything, had changed since she'd last been there. She had helped out in the cafe during her teen years, but had never actually held a job there. Gran hadn't wanted them to take money for granted, but she'd also struggled with the girls working and taking jobs from people who really needed them. To that end, they'd each had a place that called them on an emergency basis, but they were never paid for their work. The cafe had been her place, so walking into the familiar setting felt a bit like coming home.

Elsa, Ben's wife, was behind the counter and grinned broadly when she saw Violet come in. Violet pointed to an empty booth along the back wall, and Elsa nodded. She'd barely had time to slide her laptop case off her shoulder when she was enveloped in a tight hug.

"Violet May!"

Violet turned to return the embrace. "How are you, Miss Elsa?"

"I'm wonderful thanks to God's abundant blessings."

Violet smiled. The woman looked like she hadn't aged a day in ten years. "You look wonderful."

"As do you, little one." Elsa's expression saddened. "Sorry to hear about your gran. She was a good woman."

Violet nodded. "Thank you. Yes, she was."

Elsa motioned for her to sit down and then slid into the other side of the booth. "Are you in town for long?"

"I'm going to be here for a few months at least."

The twinkle in Elsa's eye warned Violet of what was coming. "You need to find a good man and settle down here."

"Still praying about that. Not many men out there like your Ben."

Elsa nodded with smile. "Yeah. God did good with my sweetheart."

"I don't want to just settle," Violet told her. "I am willing to wait for the right man."

"Always best to wait for God." Elsa reached across and patted her hand. "So what can I get you?"

"Why don't you surprise me? Never had a meal here I didn't like."

"Okay. I'll bring you something special." Elsa maneuvered herself out of the booth and headed for the kitchen.

Violet opened her case and pulled out her laptop. She had just turned it on when Elsa returned with two glasses. One with orange juice, the other with water.

"Did you see?" Elsa pointed to the clear plastic holder on the table next to the wall. "We have wireless here now. It helps bring the college students in."

Violet picked it up and smiled. "Nice. Thank you!"

Following the directions on the card in the holder, she was hooked up to the internet without a problem. Tucking one leg under her, Violet rested an elbow on the table while she began to go through her email and other social media messages.

It wasn't long before Elsa returned with a large plate filled with food. "Don't let it get cold."

Violet nodded. "I won't. It looks wonderful."

The plate held fruit in a cup, a cinnamon roll with icing, scrambled eggs, and bacon. It was more than she'd usually eat for breakfast, but she wasn't going to insult Elsa by not finishing every single bite.

∞

Dean left his office and told the guys at the front he'd be back in a bit. The air wasn't as chilly as it had been when he'd come into work a couple of hours earlier, but a cup of coffee still sounded really good. A *good* cup of coffee. Not that stuff they tried to pass off as coffee at the station. He was almost convinced they made it bad so they had an excuse to go to the cafe.

He pulled the door open and held it for the two elderly women who were exiting the restaurant.

"Thank you, Sheriff," they said in unison as they walked past him.

"You're welcome," he replied. As he walked into the inviting warmth, he took his hat off and ran a hand over his hair. He glanced around the restaurant. Almost immediately his gaze settled on the dark-haired woman sitting in a booth along the back wall. The sight of her brought a smile to his face as he approached the counter and ordered a cup of coffee.

"To go, Sheriff?" Elsa asked.

"No, I'm going to drink it here today. And could you bring me a cinnamon bun as well?"

She nodded. "A nice big one. Toasted?"

Dean grinned. "Yep! Thanks, Elsa. I'm going to talk with Miss Collingsworth."

Elsa's gaze darted to Violet and then back to him. A corner of her mouth lifted in a smile. "Great idea! I think she could use some company."

Dean wasn't sure what she meant by that, but the look in her eyes made him wonder if maybe it hadn't been such a good idea to make contact with Violet under Elsa's intense scrutiny. He took the mug of coffee she set down on the counter and made his way to where Violet sat.

She seemed intent on what she was doing, her fingers flying across the keys as she typed. A partially empty plate sat beside her laptop. Totally oblivious to his approach, she jumped when he said good morning.

Her gaze darted from him to her laptop screen before she smiled and returned the greeting.

"Mind if I sit down?" Dean asked, motioning to the empty side of the booth.

"Not at all." She smiled at him as he settled into the booth across from her. With her hair pulled back in a ponytail and her casual attire, she could easily pass for one of the college students that often frequented the restaurant.

"I didn't expect to run into you here this morning," Dean said. He took a sip of his coffee, savoring the warm burn as he swallowed.

"You and Jessa should both be happy. I brought my car to the mechanic's to get it repaired this morning. I decided to just hang out here and do a few emails and some work while I waited."

"Ah, good to hear. I wasn't going to bug you about it though. Figured you had a lot of stuff to deal with already. Though if I had heard you were planning to make any long drives, I might have gently reminded you."

Violet laughed. "Well, it will hopefully be done today, and you can cross that off your list of things to do concerning the Collingsworth girls."

Dean sobered at her comment. "Am I becoming a pest? Overstepping my bounds?"

Violet smiled and shook her head. "Not at all. With Gran gone, we probably need someone keeping track of us."

"Here you go, Sheriff." Dean looked up to see Elsa standing there with a plate. She set it down in front of him.

"Smells delicious, Elsa. Thank you."

She looked from him to Violet, and then gestured to her plate. "You're not done, are you?"

"Nope," Violet assured her. "Just taking my time."

"Good. You both enjoy," Elsa said, laying a hand on each of their shoulders before walking away.

Dean watched the older woman as she headed back to the counter, a bit surprised by the fact that she hadn't made a comment about them sitting together. A part of him kind of wished she'd said something. Maybe it would put the idea in Violet's head, because up until now, he wasn't sure she viewed him as anything other than the town's sheriff and family friend.

When he looked back at Violet, he found her watching him intently. She tore off a piece of cinnamon bun and popped it into her mouth. "Are you a regular here?"

"Yep. This is my donut shop." Dean took a bite of the warm cinnamon bun, savoring the sweetness. "Best coffee around. You're not a coffee drinker?"

"I drink it more now than I did before. Elsa apparently remembers my previous preference for orange juice."

"Did you spend a lot of time here before you left Collingsworth?" Dean stretched his legs out, bumping into her foot. He didn't immediately move, and to his surprise, neither did she.

"Yes. I used to come here to eat, but I also worked here off and on throughout my high school years."

Her phone rang, and Violet reached for it. "The garage," she said before holding it to her ear.

Dean continued eating his cinnamon bun while she talked. He saw her brow furrow and her mouth turn down. She bit her lip as she listened, and Dean worried about what they were telling her.

"And how much would that be?" She blew out a breath. "Okay. Just hold off for a bit. I'll give you a call back in a few minutes. Thank you."

She tapped the screen and laid it back on the table, her shoulders slumped.

"So what's the news?" Dean asked.

"The speedometer isn't the only thing that needs repair."

"What else is wrong?"

"To be honest, I didn't really grasp the technical terms. Something about brakes, struts and a couple of other things. The only thing that registered with me was what the bill would be."

When she told him how much it was, Dean understood why she was a little taken aback. He would have been too. "That does seem a lot of money to dump into a vehicle that age."

Violet nodded. "That was what I was thinking. I've put a lot of miles on that car. It really doesn't owe me anything, and I don't want to dump any more money into it. I was thinking about buying a new vehicle with my share of the inheritance anyway, although I had kind of hoped this one would last me until the money came through. I have some savings, but was going to use that to live on until they paid me for my next project, since I can't really pick up anything new just yet."

"Maybe Jessa would let you use Julia's car, in the meantime," Dean suggested.

"Maybe. But I noticed that Lily is kind of driving that, and I don't want to take her wheels."

"Well, if I had a spare car I'd let you use it, but I'm afraid I just have the one."

She smiled and said, "Thank you for the generous thought. I think I'll talk first with Jessa and Lily, and see if we can work something out with Gran's car. Hopefully the garage would be willing to scrap this one for me."

"I'm sure they will."

Violet turned the phone over in her hand a few times. She looked up at him, a sad smile lifting one corner of her mouth. "Who knew I'd get emotional about a car."

"From what you've said before, it sounds like that car has been more than just a mode of transportation for you," Dean pointed out. "I think it's only normal to feel something at the thought of letting it go."

Her smile broadened. "Thank you."

"For what?"

"For not laughing at me."

Dean met her gaze. "I would never laugh at you."

❧ Chapter Twelve ❧

*T*HE smile slowly slipped from her face, and for a long moment, they sat there, gazes locked. Violet's brows drew together, and she caught her lower lip between her teeth. Dean recognized the nervous gesture now and wished he could read her mind.

"More coffee?" Elsa's voice broke the connection, and Dean was kind of glad for the distraction. Something told him that Violet was aware of his interest now. Where she'd go with it, he could only hope.

"Sure. Thanks." But as she started to fill his mug, his phone rang. "Oops. Maybe not." One of his officers was calling to let him know someone was there at the office to see him. "Okay, Elsa, I'm gonna have to run." He handed her a twenty dollar bill. "That's for Violet's too. Keep the change."

Violet started to protest, but he just smiled at her. Elsa smiled too as she looked back and forth between them and said, "You're a good man, Sheriff."

"I try." As she walked away, he stood from the booth. He put his hat on and gave Violet one last smile. "Talk to you later."

"Thank you. Again."

Dean left the cafe with a flurry of butterflies in his stomach. It had been so long since he'd felt anything like it. And there was a spark of hope that maybe...just maybe...Violet was interested in him too. He shut down the little voices that echoed their same concerns after their time at the shore. If it was meant to be, things would work out.

※

Violet watched Dean walk out the door of the cafe and then glanced toward the counter where her gaze met Elsa's. Warmth gathered in her cheeks as the older woman gave her a big grin and a nod. She smiled quickly in return before turning her attention to the email she'd been working on when Dean had joined her. She'd been writing to ask her friend's advice on how to handle what she was feeling for Dean. And now she really needed that advice since it seemed that perhaps Dean was more interested than she had first thought.

She finished the email and pressed send. And then, because she'd promised Elsa, she ate the rest of the food on her plate. It wasn't an easy task, because the knot of excitement in her stomach had suppressed any appetite she might have had. Once done that, she packed up her laptop and went to say goodbye to Elsa.

"He's a good man," Elsa told her. "And I think he sees you're a good woman."

"I'm not sure-"

"Many women have tried to capture his attention, but this is the first time I've seen him seek out the attention of someone." Elsa gestured her hand to the now almost empty cafe. "He will come in and they'll invite him to sit with them, but he always sits alone or with his officers. Not today. You must be special."

"I don't know if I'm special," Violet argued. "We do have some things in common, but we've not even known each other a week. It's really too soon to know if there's something there or not."

"It's never too soon. Love can happen like that." Elsa snapped her fingers. "If he's interested, will you give him a chance?"

Violet loved Elsa, but also knew that she was a bit of a gossiper. "I will pray about it and see what happens."

Elsa sighed and shook her head. "Well, I will pray too."

With a smile, Violet leaned over to brush a kiss on the woman's cheek. "Thank you. Breakfast was wonderful."

She left the warmth of the cafe, pulling her jacket tighter when a gust of wind swept up the street. Rather than call the garage back, she was just going to go there and talk to them about making arrangements to get rid of the vehicle. She really was experiencing sadness at the thought, but it had to be done. It would be foolish to put more money into it, especially when it would just be for sentimental reasons.

This time an older gentleman was behind the counter when she walked into the office of the garage.

"Hi. I got a call a little while ago about my car."

"Violet Collingsworth?" the man asked. When she nodded, he stuck out his hand. "I'm Steve Proctor."

"Thanks for looking my car over," she said as she shook his hand.

"I wish we had better news. I would personally not recommend that you put that much money into a car this old."

"Yes, I was thinking the same thing. I've had it for almost seven years, and it has served me well. I hate to give it up, but I realize it's the smart thing to do."

"Will you have another vehicle that you can use?"

"I'm going to talk with Jessa about an option. I will eventually buy a new one, but don't want to rush into that right away." She looked over at the young man who joined them and smiled, then turned her attention back to Steve. "Will you be able to help me dispose of it?"

Steve nodded. "Yep, we can do that for you. Do you want to do it now?"

There was really no reason not to. She'd emptied the rest of her things out of the car the night before. She hadn't wanted to bring the car to the garage filled with her stuff, plus if she was hanging around for a while, there was no reason not to unpack her things. Taking a deep breath, she nodded.

For the next half hour she kept her emotions on tight rein as they went through the steps necessary for her to dispose of the car. When it was all over, she thanked them and left the garage. She stood for a minute on the street wondering what to do. She could go by Jessa's shop. Or back to the cafe or even the library. But right then, Violet just wanted to be by herself.

She slipped the strap of her laptop case over her head so that it crossed her chest and began to walk north on Main Street. There was a bit of a chill to the air, but as she kept moving, she didn't really feel it. Soon she left the town behind and settled into a moderate pace toward the manor. The tears she'd been holding back slipped silently down her cheeks. It was foolish, really, but Dean had been right when he'd said the car had been more than just a mode of transportation. That car had been with her through a lot of ups and downs, good times and bad. If she had nowhere else to go, she could always count on that car to give her a place to stay. And now it was gone. In some ways, it almost seemed like a hint of what was to come. Was this just the first of many things she would be giving up if she decided to put down roots?

She hadn't gone far when she heard the whoop of a siren behind her. Violet stepped off the road and turned to see a police car pulling up. When she spotted Dean behind the wheel, she quickly wiped her cheeks. He got out of the car and came to where she stood.

"You okay?" He reached out and brushed her cheek with his fingertips.

Violet blinked a couple of times. His tender gesture

threatened to set off another flood of tears. "I'm okay."

"I saw you leave the garage and start walking, so as soon as my meeting ended I came to see if you needed a ride."

"I don't mind the walk, but a ride would be nice too."

Dean nodded his head toward the car. "Let's go."

He walked to the passenger side of the vehicle and opened the door for her. Once she was seated, he closed the door and rounded the car to get behind the wheel. "Was Steve able to help you with disposing of it?"

"Yes. I decided to just do it now. There was no reason to wait." Violet settled back into her seat as she watched his hands grip the wheel, guiding the car onto the road.

"You could have come by and asked for a ride, you know," Dean said.

"I have no problem walking. I've walked this many times in my past. And I didn't want to take you away from anything important."

Dean glanced at her and smiled. "For some reason, this felt important to me."

Violet felt her cheeks warm at the comment. She didn't look at him when she said, "Well, thank you. I do appreciate the ride."

"And if you do need a ride any time in the future, give me a call. I can't promise I'll always be available, but if I am, I'll help you out."

Violet realized as they drove that this was the first time she'd come across someone so determined to take care of her. She'd always taken care of herself and tried to never depend on anyone else. This was new, and part of her was tempted to let him take care of her like he seemed to want to, but she was a bit concerned that there were strings attached. She didn't know what they might be exactly, but experience had shown her that often help offered so generously usually meant someone wanted something in return. It was a lesson she'd learned early on, which was why she tended not to rely on anyone else. She wanted to be able to trust that Dean wasn't going to spring anything on her, but she knew that in this instance, only time would tell.

It didn't take long for him to drive to the manor. He pulled the car around to a stop in front of the steps. He put the car in park and then turned to look at her. "So I'm wondering..."

"Wondering what?" Violet clasped her hands together in her lap. She worked to keep any expression from her face as she met his gaze.

"I know this will sound weird, but I feel like I've known you forever." Dean's brow furrowed. "I don't know if it's because I've heard about you off and on over the past few years or what, but when I look at you it doesn't seem like we just met a week ago."

"Not even a week," Violet pointed out. "Five days."

"Five days?" He lifted a brow and smiled. "See, feels like longer. I was just wondering if maybe you felt something similar."

"Yes, I feel the same way," Violet said softly. "I think maybe it's because over these past few days I've seen several different sides to you. Sides of you that, under different circumstances, would usually be seen over a longer period of time."

Dean seemed to consider that and then nodded. "You're probably right, but regardless, I wanted you to know that. To know that I...like you. I find you interesting."

Violet wasn't quite sure how to respond to that. It felt like where their relationship went from here depended a lot on her response to his statement. Everything he said, she could say back to him. It was heartwarming, and yet very scary all at the same time. She met his gaze and saw a wealth of emotion there. Hope. Vulnerability. Fear.

She loved to take risks. That feeling of flying like a bird when she'd flung herself off the bungee jump tower for the first time. The edge of fear that propelled her to paddle until her arms ached when white water rafting. It all gave her a rush that she loved. But this was different. Her life wasn't at stake, but her heart was, and for some reason, that was harder to take a risk with than life and limb.

Violet looked away, blinked a couple of times and then met Dean's gaze again. "I like you too."

Dean didn't reply right away, but she saw the fear and vulnerability leave his gaze. A small smile lifted the corners of his mouth. He tilted his head as he regarded her and said, "Are you interested in maybe seeing if there might be something more...for us?"

Violet took a deep breath and blew it out. "You know I'm not much for putting down roots, and you seem to be pretty well rooted here. I'm not sure that bodes well for us."

"I know, but I also heard you say you believed that God could change your mind if the right guy came along. I'm willing to take a chance to find out. If not, then we move on, hopefully better for having known each other. I'm not asking for you to commit to staying here in Collingsworth right at this moment. I just want a chance to see..."

"I can't make any promises, Dean." Violet looked at the manor. "To be honest, any time I did think about settling down, Collingsworth was the very last place I'd ever consider. I'm not sure that's changed."

She felt a touch on her hand and looked back at Dean. His gaze was serious as he said, "I understand that. No promises. Just friends getting to know each other better. Seeing where it might lead."

"I'd rather not have this getting to know each other process play out in front of the town. Elsa already wants to play matchmaker."

Dean nodded. "I agree. I think we could work some ways to spend time together without being in the public eye."

Violet felt a rush of relief. At least this way, if things didn't work out, their failed friendship...relationship...whatever it was, wouldn't be fodder for the gossip network of Collingsworth. "I enjoyed our talk at the lake the other day. Maybe we could meet up there again."

"Sounds good to me. I'll give you a call later."

Not sure what else to say, Violet nodded and then said goodbye as she opened the door. She fished her key out of the pocket of her laptop bag as she climbed the stairs. Before going inside, she glanced back and gave Dean a wave. He returned the wave, and as she stepped into the foyer, she heard the engine rev and then fade.

Violet closed the door and leaned back against it, her laptop bag sliding to the floor. What had she just done? She wanted a rewind button. This had to be a bad idea. And not just for her. She didn't want to hurt Dean, but right then the idea of being tied to Collingsworth wasn't exactly appealing.

God, if this is Your will, You'd better start working on that.

Picking the laptop bag by the handle, Violet made her way to the stairs and headed up to her room. She changed into a warm sweatshirt and grabbed her camera. Back down in the kitchen, she found a bottle of water in the fridge and slid it into the pocket of her hoodie. She needed the walk more than ever now. Thoughts and emotions were so jumbled up inside her. Hopefully spending some time in the nature she loved so much would give her some clarity and peace.

❧ Chapter Thirteen ❧

DEAN pointed the car back toward town, not even bothering to hide the grin on his face. For a moment there, he'd wondered if maybe he'd misread her reactions earlier that day. It was gratifying and exciting to know that it hadn't been just him. He'd seen the fear and apprehension in her eyes when he'd suggested that maybe they get to know each other better. It touched him that she'd agreed, in spite of her hesitation. And it suited him just fine to not take their...relationship public just yet. His main reason being Addy. He just didn't want her to get her hopes up and then have Violet decide that Collingsworth just wasn't where she wanted to be. He was willing to risk his own broken heart over that, but no way would he risk Addy's.

Secrets are never a good way to start a relationship. Dean heaved a sigh. He didn't intend to keep Addy from Violet for long. He just wanted to make sure that she really would give them a chance. That his being a single dad wouldn't send her running before they really had the opportunity to get to know each other. Resolutely silencing the voice in his head, Dean focused on when they'd next be able to spend some time together. Most likely it would depend more on his schedule since he had a full-time job that demanded his attention, and he didn't want to take too much time away from Addy either.

After he pulled into his spot in front of the sheriff's office, he took a minute to compose himself and switch gears. He didn't want to walk into the building grinning like an idiot. Business first, pleasure later. But at least he had hope, and he could live with that for now.

༄

They weren't able to get together again until Saturday afternoon, but Dean had called each night around ten so they could talk. The first couple of nights had been a bit awkward, and the calls had been short, but by the time Friday arrived, they had gotten to where they were talking for almost an hour. Violet felt more at ease and was ready to spend some time with him in person.

"Going out?" Jessa asked when Violet came into the kitchen dressed in her hiking clothes.

She set her small backpack on the counter. "Yep. Feel the need for something more than just a casual walk. I'll probably be gone for two or three hours." She patted her sweatshirt's pocket. "I have my cell phone though, so if you need me, just call."

"Sounds good. I'm heading into the shop for bit. Rose will go with me. I think Lily is going bowling with her friends."

"Nate too?" Violet asked.

"Yes. I believe so."

"Are you okay with that?" She pulled a couple of bottles of water out of the fridge and put them in the backpack. The day before she'd made a trip into town and picked up some snack foods for the hike, and they were already in the backpack.

"Yes. As long as she follows the guidelines we agreed on, I'm not going to give her any grief."

"I'm glad you're giving her a chance. I wish Gran had done that with you and Lance."

Jessa's movements stilled. "Yeah, well in that case, I think Gran was right. I heard he got engaged not long after Gran made me stop seeing him. So much for his undying love."

Violet winced at the bitterness in Jessa's voice. Was this why she'd never gone on to date anyone else? "Hopefully it will be different for Lily."

"She's too young to be getting serious anyway. I hope Nate respects that."

"I think he will."

Rose skipped into the kitchen carrying a pink backpack. "I got my tablet to play with while you work, Jessa."

Violet let the subject drop and smiled at the young girl. "Do you like going to Jessa's shop?"

She nodded. "Sometimes they let me put things in the bags for the customers."

"Well, you have fun." Violet pressed a kiss to her satiny blond hair. "I'll see you at supper."

The afternoon was warm until she walked into the forest. The shaded air held a touch of chill, but she had dressed for that and knew she'd heat up as she hiked. She'd told Dean she'd be at the shore around one-thirty. Her excitement made her move more quickly through the forest than she might have otherwise. Usually her hikes were about the journey not the destination, but today she had a definite goal that drew her.

She was a little out of breath as she neared the lake just over thirty minutes later. Not wanting to arrive huffing and puffing, Violet took a few minutes to rest before walking the last leg of the hike at a more leisurely pace.

She spotted Dean right away as she stepped from the forest to the clearing. He stood with his back to her, looking out over the lake. She paused to drink in the sight of him. He wasn't wearing a hat, so she could see his dark, closely cropped hair that was styled most likely as a result of his job. His feet were braced apart, and his black leather jacket was pushed back where his hands were in the pockets of his jeans. Strength and confidence radiated from him, and Violet found herself drawn to it. She wondered what it would be like to be held in his arms, close to his firm chest.

Unconsciously she took a step in his direction and must have made a sound, because he turned toward her. He wore sunglasses that shielded his eyes, but his smile was warm. As she walked to where he stood, he took the glasses off and slipped them into the inside pocket of his jacket. She felt a bit underdressed in her worn jeans and hoodie compared to his dark jeans, white button up shirt and leather jacket.

"Hey," he said as she came to a stop next to him. "How was the walk?"

"Very nice." Violet looked out over the lake, fighting the swarm of nervous butterflies in her stomach. "Any time I can be outdoors is usually a good time."

"I hear you," Dean agreed.

Standing next to him, Violet understood why Jessa considered Dean short. At five-eleven, a guy needed to be at least a couple of inches over six feet for Jessa to feel comfortable with them. Dean was probably right around six feet which put him a good five inches taller than her.

"Want to sit down?" Dean gestured behind him. "I brought a couple of folding lawn chairs that might be more comfortable than the rock."

Violet nodded. "That sounds good. My legs are ready for a rest."

"I don't mind the hike, but my aging body doesn't like the rock much for sitting." He set up both chairs facing the lake, and motioned for her to take one. "These might not be the most comfortable, but they were light enough to carry for the bit I had to walk."

"They're great," Violet said as she sank down onto the fabric seat. "And what's with the aging body comment? You're not that old."

Dean sat down and stretched his legs out. "I'll be forty on my next birthday."

Violet shot him a surprised look. "Really? I never would have guessed. You're ten years older than me."

Without looking at her, Dean asked, "Is that going to be a problem?"

"No. Not at all," Violet assured him. "I hadn't really thought about it, but I wouldn't have guessed your age from looking at you."

Dean looked at her then and winked. "I get good aging genes from my dad."

"I wish I knew more about my dad," Violet said as she pulled out a water bottle. She held it to Dean. "Want one?"

He took the bottle from her and opened the cap while she did the same with hers. She took a deep swallow, staring out at the water.

"Do you know anything at all about him?"

Violet ran her finger along the ridged edge of the bottle. "No. And Mama never listed fathers on the birth certificates. Most likely the guys she was hanging with wouldn't have cared one way or the other about having fathered a child."

"So none of you know your fathers?"

"I don't think so. Well, we have an idea who Rose's is. And I'm pretty sure Gran knew who Jessa's father was since Mama got pregnant with her while here in Collingsworth, but I don't know if she ever told Jessa."

"Have you ever thought about trying to find out?"

Violet shrugged. "I do wonder at times, but right now I'm more interested in finding Mama. I figure that if she's still...able, she'd have the answers. I have vague memories of a man who was around in the year before Mama had Cami. I think that perhaps he was her father, but I can't say for sure." She glanced at Dean. "Do you have siblings?"

"I did." His jaw tightened. "A sister."

"You did?" Violet debated probing, but figured that's what these times together were for—to get to know each other. "What happened to her?"

"She was killed in a random shooting about four years ago."

Violet turned in her chair so she could see him. She pulled one leg up and wrapped her arms around it. "That's horrible."

Dean stared down at the ground. "It was a rough time. I was supposed to be testifying in a high profile case. I'm still not convinced it wasn't connected."

"They never caught who did it?"

He shook his head. "One of the most frustrating things in my life. I was a detective and couldn't solve the mystery of my own sister's death."

"So it's a cold case now?"

"It will never be solved. There were no witnesses. The only chance is if they happen to use the same gun again and get caught, but something tells me that won't happen."

Violet reached over and laid her hand on his arm. "I'm sorry that your family had to go through something like that."

"It's one of the reasons I ended up here. Your grandmother came to me after it happened and asked me if wanted a change in my life. A more peaceful place to live. Safer. I worked the first six months as deputy sheriff and then stepped in as acting sheriff until she talked me into running for the position in the election. The rest is history."

"Do you regret your move here?"

Dean shook his head. "Not at all. I was getting burned out. I made detective pretty young after I got my degree, and then they started sending me undercover. My young appearance made me ideal to send into situations where they needed a younger, but experienced, cop. It was wearing on me, and after almost having an undercover operation go south in the worst way, I decided to move on. This gives me the opportunity to still do a job I love without the high stress levels of what I was doing in Minneapolis." He looked over and grinned at her. "Honestly, Cami's little stunt was the most excitement we'd had so far this month."

Violet shuddered. "I still don't know what she was thinking. I'm kind of afraid to ask her."

"Best to let sleeping dogs lie," Dean suggested.

"Oh, that's definitely my plan," Violet assured him.

The sun moved across the sky as they continued to talk. Violet dug out some of the snacks she'd brought. She offered him a granola bar when the conversation turned to movies and television shows they enjoyed, and then shared trail mix as the conversation veered into music.

"I'm a big gospel music fan," Violet admitted.

"I was raised with that kind of music. And lots of traditional hymns. I'm glad the church here usually has a good mix in the music they select for their services. What's your church like for music?"

"My church?" Violet asked.

"Well, the one you attend in Seattle."

Violet let out a sigh. "I'm not really a regular church attender."

Dean's brows drew together. "You aren't? I guess I just assumed... I mean, I saw you at church on Sunday."

Violet nodded. "Oh, I believe in God. Just with my traveling, I had a hard time finding a church that I felt comfortable in. But that doesn't mean I don't worship or have a relationship with God."

"So you're not opposed to a structured church environment?"

"Not at all. Personally though, for the past few years I've adopted that verse in the Bible that talks about where two or three are gathered in God's name, that He is in their midst." Violet rubbed a hand on her thigh. "There is a group of us in and around Seattle who hike and climb together regularly. Most of us are Christians, so we make it part of our outings to study the Bible, pray together and, of course, sing. We have a bit of an outreach with other outdoor enthusiasts. There's nothing wrong with worshipping in a church building with a structured service, but I tell you, sitting out in God's creation to sing, worship and pray just makes me feel that much closer to Him."

"I can see how that might be. There are times I've brought my Bible on my hikes and spent my devotional time out in nature. There are no distractions, and you're right, being in His creation does remind me of how awesome and powerful He is. I wasn't involved as much with church in Minneapolis as my schedule was crazy, and to be honest, there were times I wasn't all that interested. However, since moving here I've been able to attend regularly, and it has definitely had a positive impact on my spiritual life."

"I attended every Sunday and Wednesday when I was in high school, and will attend while I'm living here now." Violet heard a beep on her phone and pulled it out. She sighed. "I guess I'd better head home. I promised the girls I'd be back for supper."

"Yeah. I need to get going as well." He stood up and then held out his hand.

Violet hesitated before slipping her hand into his. Dean's grip was strong as he pulled her to her feet. The movement brought them close, and they stood that way for a long moment before he released her, and Violet stepped back.

"I really enjoyed this afternoon," Dean said. "I hope you did as well."

"I did. I needed this," Violet told him. "It's been a long week, and this was a nice end to it. Guess I'll see you at church tomorrow?"

Dean shook his head. "Sorry. I'm actually driving into the Twin Cities tonight to spend a little time with my parents. I'll be back late tomorrow night."

Violet tried to ignore the disappointment that flooded her at the news she wouldn't see him the next day. "I'm sure they'll enjoy that."

"I try to get down there once a month or so. Sometimes they come up this way as well." Dean picked up her backpack from the ground and held it out to her. "I probably won't get a chance to talk to you again until Monday. I hope you have a good day tomorrow."

"I'm sure I will." She held out her left hand, palm down, toward him. When he took it in his right hand and squeezed it, she said, "Drive safe."

"I will," he assured her with a small smile. He ran his thumb over the back of her hand then let it slide from his.

Violet felt his gaze on her as she turned to walk to the opening in the trees that led to her path into the woods. Her steps home weren't as quick as the ones that had brought her earlier, since she really was reluctant to leave Dean. Talking with him had been interesting and fun. They hadn't agreed on everything, but it seemed they held the same things as important. For the first time Violet let herself seriously consider that maybe this was the man God had for her. It was still soon, but so far she found herself more attracted to him each time they talked or spent time together. As the manor came into view, Violet paused and said a prayer, asking God to give her and Dean wisdom with regards to whatever was developing between them.

❧ Chapter Fourteen ❧

DEAN made quick work of the trail that led back to the house. He felt bad that Violet had the longer walk, but she didn't seem to mind. Once back at the house, he gathered up the bags he'd packed earlier for him and Addy and put them in the SUV. He drove into town to pick her up at her friend's house where she'd spent the afternoon.

"McDonald's for supper, Daddy?" Addy asked from the back seat.

"Sounds good to me!" Dean pulled through the drive-thru of the fast food restaurant. As he waited for the food, he put on the DVD Addy requested for the drive. He thanked God for whoever had suggested adding DVD players in vehicles. These trips to Minneapolis were much easier for Addy with something to entertain her.

Once they had their food, he pulled into a parking spot and got out. He opened the rear door and made sure that Addy was secure in her booster in the middle of the back seat. Too many years of attending accidents where children were injured because they were incorrectly buckled into their seats had made him paranoid about Addy's safety in the car. He put her drink in the cup holder of her seat and gave her the bag that held her food. Because he'd heard the movie she'd chosen one too many times, when she requested the headset, he willingly gave it to her.

"All set?" he asked the little girl who was looking more and more like his sister every day.

"Yep." She gave him a big grin and a thumbs up.

He settled behind the wheel and got his own meal situated so it didn't require his attention once he was on the road. Before backing out of the spot, he plugged his phone into the stereo so he could listen to his play list then checked to make sure his hands free device was working correctly. People might call him paranoid, but having already lost a loved one, he did his best to travel safely, especially when he had Addy with him.

Once on the road, his thoughts drifted to the afternoon with Violet. It had gone better than anticipated. Their time together had passed by too quickly though, and he couldn't wait until the next time he could see her. The afternoon visit had just added to his conviction that there was something special between them. He hoped that Violet felt the same way. He thought maybe she did. Holding her hand in his just before she'd left had stirred up emotions in him, and he'd had to fight the urge to not let her go.

He hadn't decided yet if he was going to mention her to his folks or not. They always told him they were praying that he'd find someone to love. Someone who would stick by his side this time. Dean hadn't been actively praying for that. However, Addy made up for it as she prayed for a mama each night in her prayers.

In spite of his own thoughts on the subject, it appeared God had dropped the answer to his parents' and Addy's prayer right in front of him. But he figured he'd wait to say anything until Violet gave him a more definitive sign about how she felt. He may not have been praying for someone to love before, but he sure was now.

❧

Sunday and Monday dragged for Violet. The only highlight was when her best friend from Seattle chose to call in response to her email instead of just hitting reply. They talked late into the night Sunday, and Lucy had been happy to give some advice based on her own experiences. But more than that, she'd just been so excited that Violet had finally found someone that made her think more seriously about settling down. Lucy's excitement was contagious, and Violet found herself getting even more caught up in it as they talked. They'd also discussed wedding plans, and when Violet intended to arrive.

Monday morning Violet had to fight the urge to go into town and see if Dean was there. Instead she tried to keep herself busy editing pictures that she hoped to submit with an article in a couple of weeks. Mid-afternoon her phone rang. She looked at the display and let out a quick breath when she saw Tom's name on the screen.

"Hey, little lady." Tom said when she answered the phone. "Just wanted to touch base with you."

"Thanks for calling. How has it been going?" Violet knew it was probably too soon to expect any real answers, but she couldn't help but hope for that.

"I'm still working my way through all the information you sent me. I've found a few people who remember her, but nothing recent. No one seems to have had any contact with her after she got pregnant with Lily."

Violet felt her stomach clench. "Do you think that means something happened to her?"

"Right now I'm going to assume that I just haven't asked the right questions of the right people. It does seem she dropped off the face of the earth right around that time though. However, it could just mean that when she left Collingsworth that last time, she moved to a completely new place you didn't know about."

"I sure hope that's the case. Will you be able to find her though? If that's what she did?"

"No one can ever completely disappear. At least none that

I've had experience with. If she's out there to be found, I will find her. It just may take a bit longer than I thought now that the information well seems to have dried up."

Disappointment coursed through Violet. "Thank you for your help with this. Do you need some money to help with expenses?"

Initially Tom said he didn't, but then after a little more discussion, they settled on an amount that worked for both of them. This search was another reason Violet hadn't rushed out to buy another car. She wanted to make sure she had the money available to continue the search. That was more important than a car right now.

After she ended her conversation with Tom, Violet pushed away from the table and went to stand at the kitchen window looking out over the back yard. She remembered her mom talking to her about when she'd been a little girl at the manor. Her favorite spot had been out in the yard. Her dad had built her a tire swing, and she'd loved to swing on it. *Free like a bird!* That's how she used to describe the feeling she'd had when swinging. She'd been so desperate for freedom. And for love. Violet hoped that she'd found both wherever she was now.

Violet turned from the window and went back to the computer. Maybe, just maybe, it was time to ask Stan again if he knew where her mother was. Last time she'd asked, he given her the ambiguous response that there was no information he could give her. She'd interpreted that to mean that his loyalty lay with Julia, and he couldn't tell her anything. But now with Julia gone...

She picked up her phone and found him in her contact list. As it rang, she walked through the house to the living room and the front window where she could see if Jessa arrived home. It rang four times before a female voice answered it. She was a bit confused when the woman gave the name of Stan's firm as part of her greeting, because Violet thought she'd been calling his cell phone.

"Hi. This is Violet Collingsworth. I'd like to speak with Stan please."

"Oh, I'm sorry. Stan is out of the office for the next couple of weeks. Could one of the other partners help you?"

"No, thanks. I just need to speak with him."

"I'll make note that you called, and he can get back to you when he's in the office next."

Disappointment weighed on Violet as she turned from the window and went back to her laptop. She sat for a few minutes, phone in hand, staring blankly at the screen. She had hoped that maybe Stan could give her a lead to pass on to Tom. Now it was just going to be more waiting. Normally a patient person, this was trying for her. She just felt like the waiting had dragged on for so long now.

When Jessa got home with the girls a little while later, Violet asked her if she knew that Stan was away.

"Yes," Jessa said as she emptied the grocery bags she'd brought home. "He called me on Thursday to remind me he and his family were leaving for a planned cruise for two weeks. He wanted to make sure we didn't need anything before he left. When Gran died, he offered to postpone the trip, but I told him that as long as we had the will reading before he left, anything else could wait until he got back." She paused and glanced at Violet. "Did you need something?"

"I just wanted to run something by him. It can wait." It wasn't like she had any choice now.

Though she would have loved to talk to Jessa about what she had started with Tom, Violet was pretty sure what her older sister's response would be. It wasn't until later that night when Dean called that she was finally able to talk about it.

"So Tom said his leads had dried up?" Dean said when she told him about her conversation with the older man.

"Yeah. He said it's like she vanished off the face of the earth after dropping Lily off. I tried calling the lawyer today to see if maybe he'd spill something now that Gran was gone, but he's on vacation."

"Seems odd he'd take vacation so soon after her death," Dean commented.

"Jessa said they'd had a family cruise planned for quite a while. He offered to postpone it, but she told him to go ahead and go, and that we'd deal with anything that came up when he got back." Violet turned onto her side, snuggling beneath her blanket. "I'm just praying that something comes through for Tom in the meantime."

"If there's anything out there to be found, he'll find it. It might take some time, but Tom will find it."

Dean's word reassured Violet, and she felt the disappointment from earlier ease away. "How was your visit with your parents?"

Their conversation continued as Dean shared about his time in the Twin Cities. And as part of that he shared a bit more about his family and their history. She found it interesting to hear about such a normal family. It was so different from what she'd known. It would definitely be how she'd like to raise her children...if she ever had any.

In the darkness of her room, Violet felt herself drifting off. Not wanting to fall asleep mid-conversation, she told Dean she needed to go.

"If you happen to wander into town in the next day or two, feel free to stop by the office," Dean said.

"I might just do that. I can only take so much time in the Manor."

After he said good night, Violet slid her phone onto the bed next to her and curled up under the covers. The way she felt after each interaction with Dean was getting stronger and more intense. The last image she saw before slipping into sleep was the way he'd looked at her at the lake.

৩৵৵

Dean had hoped that Violet might take him up on his invitation to stop by the next day, but she didn't show. When he phoned that night she told him that Rose hadn't been feeling well, so she'd offered to stay with her while Jessa went to the shop.

"I'm not sure if she was really sick, or if it was something she was trying to avoid at school," Violet said with a chuckle. "Having done the avoid school thing, you'd think I'd be able to tell, but she's good."

Dean almost said he knew what that was like, but then bit his tongue. It was getting harder for him to keep Addy out of their conversations. But he really, really wanted to make sure that she felt enough for him that the presence of Addy in his life wouldn't scare her off. In a small town like this, though, with him so well known to the family, someone was bound to mention Addy sooner or later. Dean knew he needed to make the decision to tell her before that happened.

The next morning Dean was in the middle of a phone call with a detective in a neighboring town talking about a case that involved both their forces when he spotted Violet walk in the door of the office. She spoke to the deputy at the desk who let her through. The officers all knew that if a Collingsworth showed up they were to be shown to his office.

With the phone still pressed to his ear, Dean stood up and motioned Violet in when the deputy brought her to his door. He covered the receiver with his hand and said, "Have a seat. I'll just be another minute."

Violet nodded and smiled as she sat down in the chair. He settled back into his seat, running a hand across his hair as he listened to the other man's explanation of his team's involvement. It took more than a minute to come to agreement on a flow of information and evidence, but thankfully the other man was as eager as he was to get this case tied up.

"Okay, thanks, George. I'll pass the information on to the deputies involved," Dean said and then ended the call. As he hung up, he smiled at Violet. "I'm glad you stopped by. How are you doing?"

"Good." She shifted in her seat, crossing one denim clad leg over the other. She wore a light pink sweater that accented her tanned skin and dark hair and eyes. "I had to come in to do some business at the bank, so thought I'd take you up on your offer."

"I'm glad you did. It feels like forever since I saw you."

"It was only Saturday," Violet reminded him, her full lips curving into a small smile. "But yes, it does feel like longer than that."

"Are you interested in going out for dinner?" Dean asked. He hadn't planned to ask so soon, but he wasn't going to wait until the weekend to spend time with her.

Her brow furrowed. "Are you sure that's a good idea?"

"We don't have to go to dinner here in town. If you don't mind a bit of a drive, we could go to the next town."

"I'll have to give Jessa a reason for being gone for the evening." Violet bit her lower lip. "But I think I can figure something out. Should I meet you here in town?"

"Sounds good." Dean felt excitement arc through him. It was the first time he'd been out on a date in a long time. He felt a bit like a teenager. "I'm off work at five so any time after that."

"I'll be here." Violet smiled at him, and Dean knew he would gladly spend the rest of his life trying to keep that smile on her face.

She didn't stay too long, but Dean had a hard time concentrating on his work after that. He did remember to phone Miss Sylvia and ask her to please keep Addy for dinner and possibly put her to bed if he wasn't home in time. She usually met Addy's bus each day and then cooked dinner for them, but Dean would take over after that. It was rare he wasn't there for bedtime, but it did happen occasionally. Miss Sylvia assured him that she'd take good care of Addy, and he knew she would.

Now he just had to make it through the rest of the day.

✎ *Chapter Fifteen* ✎

JESSA told her to take the car without asking any further questions. Violet couldn't believe it was that easy, but she didn't bother to offer any reason for needing the car. She'd learned early on she could talk herself into corners by over-explaining to someone who hadn't asked for an explanation.

It took a while to figure out what to wear. Not that she had a lot of choice. Her wardrobe consisted mainly of jeans, sweatshirts and sweaters. She settled on a black blazer over a lavender tank top with embellishments on the front. Her dressiest pants were a pair of fitted black jeans that she tucked into her knee high black boots that had a bit of a heel which gave her some height. Thankfully, while they were living together Lucy had made sure Violet knew how to apply at least a minimum of makeup and told her to use a straightener on her already straight hair to make it silky and shiny.

Bracing herself for questions from Jessa on the way out, Violet was relieved when the only person she ran into was Lily.

"Wow! You look nice," she said when Violet went into the

kitchen to get the car keys.

"Thanks." She figured if her teenage sister thought she looked nice that she at least would pass muster on a date.

"Going out for dinner?" Lily asked and then gave her a sly smile. "A date?"

"Just spending some time with a friend," Violet told her.

"Uh huh." Lily had a knowing look in her eye. "Anyone I know?"

"Probably, but I'm not going to tell you."

Lily laughed. "Like you'll be able to keep that secret in this town."

"Well, if you don't say anything to Jessa, you'll be the first I'll tell...if there's anything to tell."

Lily laid a hand on her heart. "I promise to keep my mouth shut."

"Good girl!" Violet pressed a kiss to her cheek. "See you later."

Once in town she parked near the cafe instead of the sheriff's office. She texted Dean to let him know she was there and then waited in the car until she saw him step out the door of the station. Taking a deep breath, she picked up her purse from the passenger seat and got out. She locked the car and then turned to see Dean waiting for her next to his SUV. Looking both ways, she quickly crossed the street. He had the passenger side door open for her as she approached.

She felt a little silly sneaking around, but was glad when he closed her door.

"You look beautiful," he said as he backed the vehicle out of his parking spot.

"Thank you," Violet said, warmth flooding her cheeks. "And you look very handsome yourself. Do you keep a change of clothes at work?"

"Yep. You never know when I might need them."

He wore the same leather jacket he'd had on the day

they'd met at the lake. Instead of jeans though, his cream colored shirt was tucked into a pair of black slacks. And her stomach did a flip when she got a whiff of his cologne. Her excitement level climbed with every minute they were together.

"I hope you're okay if the place we're going isn't super fancy," Dean said as he turned the car onto the highway.

Violet laughed. "Do I strike you as someone who is more comfortable in fancy environments? Simple is good."

He glanced at her and smiled. "That's what I like to hear. The food is good though."

It took about thirty minutes to get to the next town. He pulled into a parking lot beside a large building. He laid a hand on her back as they walked into the pub-style restaurant. The hostess showed them to a booth right away. It was along the side of the restaurant where windows lined the wall, but the high backs of the booth seats gave them privacy. Violet slid into one side, tucking her leg up under her.

"Nervous?" Dean asked as he settled across the table from her.

"That obvious?"

"Well, I know I am, so I figured maybe if you were too, it would make things easier." He paused when the waitress arrived at their table. She took their drink orders and then left them. "I haven't been on a date in...forever."

"Yeah, my dates have been few and far between, but I never felt like this about any of them."

Dean tilted his head. "I guess I never asked if you were already involved with someone. I'm going to assume that you would have said something if you were."

Violet nodded. "Yes, I would have. There isn't anyone."

The bluesy music filled the silence as they looked at their menus.

"What do you recommend?" Violet asked, assuming Dean had been there before since he'd said the food was good.

"I've only been here once before, so I can't really give any tried and true recommendations. Maybe we can ask the waitress when she comes back."

The waitress was more than happy to help them out and soon left with their orders. Violet looked around the restaurant, appreciative of the atmosphere. The lights hanging low over each table gave a cozy feeling. And as she settled back against the booth, she felt herself relaxing.

As the evening progressed, Violet was surprised that they never seemed to run out of things to talk about. Not that there weren't lulls in their conversation, but neither of them seemed pressured to fill the silence. He was winning over more and more of her heart each time she was with him. And she found the thought of settling in Collingsworth wasn't the death knell it had once been. Maybe she could make a home here after all. With this man.

❦

Dean didn't want the evening to end, but didn't want to be too late getting home. Around eight he suggested they head back to town. The flash of disappointment on Violet's face encouraged him. At least he wasn't the only one who didn't want the evening to end. He knew he had to tell her about Addy soon, but tonight he wanted it to be just about the two of them.

After paying the bill, he led the way out of the restaurant. He took her hand to help her step over a concrete abutment, but didn't release her right away, and she made no move to end the contact. They walked hand in hand to where the car was, and Dean wished he'd parked a few blocks away. Once they were on the highway back to town, he laid his hand on the console between them, palm up. It took a few seconds, but then he felt her slide her fingers through his.

They didn't talk much on the trip back to Collingsworth, and he finally had to relinquish her hand in order to maneuver the turns once they turned off the highway. Main Street was dimly lit, but there was still enough light for people to recognize them as he pulled in next to her car.

"Thank you for this evening," Dean said.

"Thank *you*," Violet said with emphasis. "I really enjoyed it."

"I know it's still soon, but do you think there's a chance that you might be inclined to take this a little more seriously?" Dean found he was tiring of the covert meetings. He wanted to be able to be around her in public and have people know they were a couple. The feelings he'd experienced during their first meeting had only grown stronger. They weren't going away.

"Do you mean taking it public?" Violet asked.

"Among other things," Dean said. If she was willing to go public with it that would show him she was taking it seriously, and hopefully wouldn't be scared off by finding out about Addy.

"I think so. I'm just still...scared." He heard a tremor in her voice.

"Scared of what?"

"Well, it's clear my mom wasn't very good with relationships. Gran didn't seem to fare much better, even though she did get married. I just don't want to parade it out in public for people to gossip and dissect."

"You want to wait until you're one hundred percent sure?" Dean asked. "At some point, keeping this private will bring about more gossip than going public."

Violet sighed. "Yes, I know. Give me another day or two, okay?"

Dean reached out and brushed her cheek with his fingertips. "If that's what you need, that's what you'll get."

"Thank you." Dean heard the relief in her voice and hoped it really would only be a day or two.

They said their goodnights, and then Violet got out of his car into hers. He followed her out of town to the turn where she went one way and he went the opposite. He wished she'd been more willing to make their relationship official. It made him reluctant to tell her about Addy because clearly she wasn't feeling as confident of things between them as he was. He'd give her two days, and then he'd be revisiting the subject.

❧ Chapter Sixteen ❧

OVER the next two days, Violet had plenty of time to try to figure out her reluctance to agree to Dean's request that they go public with their budding relationship. It was hard to pinpoint it to one thing, but ever since high school she'd been an intensely private person. Being a member of the richest family in town, Violet had never known for sure that the girls who befriended her were interested in her as a person or because of the Collingsworth wealth. One time she'd felt comfortable enough to share who she liked with a girl who claimed to be her best friend, only to have it spread all across the school. From that point on, she was extremely cautious about who she shared what with.

Lucy Duncan had barged into her life one weekend and had not given her a chance to keep her defenses up. She'd been persistent and friendly until Violet finally gave in and let her walls down. Lucy was the one person Violet trusted completely—even more than her sisters. So when Lucy told her to give it a chance, to take the risk of going public even if it did fail, Violet decided it was time to put aside her fears and do just that.

She also knew that going public would be putting it out

there that she was considering a permanent move back to Collingsworth. That would probably come as much of a shock to some as her being in a relationship with the sheriff. Thankfully she'd get a break from any scrutiny next week when she flew to Seattle for Lucy's wedding. Kind of put it out there and then disappear for a few days. Not that she was thrilled at the idea of leaving Dean right then, but she wouldn't miss her friend's wedding for anything. Plans had been made for her to fly out on the next Tuesday so she could help with last minute things for the Friday night wedding. She planned to fly back on Saturday afternoon. Jessa had agreed to let her take the car and just leave it in long term parking for the five days she'd be gone.

On Wednesday morning, Violet took the car into town with the sole purpose of talking with Dean. He'd given her space to think and pray about things. Aside from a couple of texts he hadn't called or made arrangements to meet. Violet wondered if maybe he might be entertaining second thoughts about having a relationship with such a skittish chick.

Once in town she parked outside the library. She pulled out her cell phone and sent him a text to see if she could stop by. When he didn't reply right away, Violet gathered up her stuff and went into the library. She knew he was a busy man, so when a little voice tried to convince her he was ignoring or avoiding her, Violet pushed it aside.

She'd been in the library about fifteen minutes when her phone vibrated an alert. The screen showed that Dean had replied to her message, saying she could come any time. She texted back that she'd be there in a couple of minutes and then gathered up her things. Her stomach was knotted as she walked down the street from the library to the sheriff's office.

The same deputy from the other day was seated behind the desk and waved her through. "Good morning, Miss Collingsworth."

"Morning!"

"The sheriff said to go on in when you got here," the young man told her.

Thanking him with a smile, Violet made her way to Dean's office. He stood as she walked in, and her heart skipped a beat. He smiled at her in such a way that Violet knew for certain he hadn't been avoiding her.

"It's great to see you," he said as he came around the desk to where she stood.

Violet hesitated for just a second, then stepped close and slid her hand into his. "It's good to see you too."

He gave her hand a gentle squeeze. "I was hoping you hadn't run off on me."

Violet shook her head. "No, just needed to get over a few issues I have with regards to having my personal life out in public. Nothing like dating the sheriff to thrust yourself in the spotlight. Especially in this town."

"I understand," Dean said with a warm smile that lit up his eyes.

Someone cleared their throat, and Violet let her hand slide from Dean's as she turned.

"Sorry to interrupt, Sheriff," a middle aged woman said, "but I have a message for you."

"No problem, Cecily. What's up?"

The woman's gaze moved back and forth between the two of them, filled with curiosity, until it settled on Dean. "Addy's teacher, Mrs. Davenport, called from the school to remind you about Friday. Apparently Addy asked her to call because, and I quote, 'Daddy forgets stuff sometimes'."

Violet felt the breath slam out of her. *Daddy?* She took a step to the side so she was shielded by Dean's body from the woman's gaze. Confusion filled her mind as she tried to think of reasons why some child would refer to him as Daddy...other than the obvious one.

"Thanks, Cecily. I have it marked on my calendar."

Violet didn't see the woman leave, but she heard Dean shut the door and then it was just a very loud, very awkward silence in the room with them.

Dean sighed. "Look, I-"

"Daddy?" Violet forced the word passed the tightness in her throat. "You have a child?"

Dean rubbed his forehead. "Yes, but it's a long story. I was going to tell-"

Violet cut him off. "You don't think maybe that was something you should have mentioned on the very first day? That's not a small detail. You had no right to ask me to consider a relationship with you, and then leave out that one very important detail. No right!"

Struggling to keep the tears at bay, Violet took a couple of deep breaths. Dean stood watching her, pain on his face. "I'm sorry, Violet. I was just..."

She pressed a hand to her stomach. "No. I trusted you. Just...no." Pain lashed at her heart like a whip. Each stinging strike ripping at her. "I need to go."

"Violet, please, let me explain," Dean said, grabbing her arm as she moved passed him toward the door. "I was going to tell you."

She looked back at him, her hand gripping the door knob. "Too late. If we don't have trust, we don't have anything."

His hand slid from her arm when, with a deep breath and a determination to maintain her composure, Violet opened the door and walked out of his office. Drawing on every last ounce of strength she had, she pasted a smile on her face and nodded to the officer who'd let her in earlier.

"Have a good day," she said to him. She used her shoulder to push open the door. As she stepped into the bright, cool spring day, Violet felt as if her whole world had just shifted. Her steps felt so unsteady she wondered if people might look at her and think she was drunk. She moved as quickly as she could, desperately needing to get to her car and to the manor. She doubted Dean would chase her, but on the off chance he did, she wanted to be gone.

At the car, she fumbled to push the right button on the fob to unlock the door. Once it was open, she allowed herself a glance toward the sheriff's office. There was one final lash of pain across her heart when she saw Dean standing on the top step, hands on his hips watching her. When he saw her look his way, he took a step down, but hands shaking, she quickly slid behind the wheel and jabbed the key into the ignition.

When she looked in her rear view mirror as she pulled away, she saw that Dean now stood on the sidewalk, but wasn't moving in her direction any longer. Violet shut down all thought and emotion as she drove.

The manor was silent when she let herself in. She hoped that meant everyone was gone, because she really needed to just be alone. Without much thought, she grabbed the hoodie she'd left on a chair earlier and pulled it on. She shoved a bottle of water into the front pocket and left the house. In the past, the rock at the lake shore had been her destination when she'd needed alone time, but she didn't dare go there today. If Dean did come looking for her, that would be the first place he'd look. Instead, she took the path that led right to the lake behind the house and then headed in the opposite direction along the shoreline.

Though she managed to keep her thoughts from overwhelming her, she couldn't keep her emotions at bay. Tears streamed down her face as she walked. *Why?* It was the one thing she just couldn't figure out. Why wouldn't he have told her sooner? She could have understood that he might not have told her right away about a previous marriage. That was in his past, after all. But a child? That wasn't just a part of his past, but also his present and his future. Their future.

The rocks on the beach rolled beneath her feet and made walking more challenging, but Violet trudged on until she came to a widening in the shore line. A large log sat on a slight incline up from the water. Wearily she made her way over to it and sank down on its rough surface. She drew her knees close and wrapped her arms tightly around them. Staring out at the lake, she listened to the soft lapping of the water along the shoreline, craving the peace that the sounds of nature usually gave her. Unfortunately today, that serenity didn't come.

Tears continued to fall. Was there something wrong with her that Dean had thought it best not to tell her right away about his daughter? To be honest, she hadn't thought seriously about having children herself. When one wasn't sure about settling down, they really weren't sure about having children. That had been her mindset for many years. But now she had a relationship and a child dropped in her lap and had no idea what to do about it.

Taking a chance on a relationship with a single guy had been one thing. If things didn't work out, she would have just moved on, as would have he. But now, with a child involved, they couldn't just have a casual relationship to see if it might work for them. She had no idea how old...Addy was, but she was in school, so no doubt the little girl understood the ramifications of her daddy having a girlfriend.

Violet laid her cheek on her knees. If she'd been confused and uncertain about the relationship before this revelation, she was doubly so now. She had absolutely no idea what to do. What stung the most was that Dean hadn't trusted her with such an important piece of information. She felt worthless, like he hadn't deemed her worthy enough yet to be told about his daughter. Had she jumped through the final hoop today when she'd agreed to go public with their relationship?

Maybe he'd done it to protect his daughter. That made some sense, but if he knew anything about her, he would have realized that if he had wanted to wait to introduce the two of them, she would have understood. He hadn't needed to hide that part of his life from her.

Ugh! Violet pressed the heels of her hands against her eyes. She needed time to think. Time away from everything here. Maybe leaving sooner than planned for Seattle might be a good thing. Because now, aside from figuring out how she felt about Dean, she really did need to think about taking on a ready-made family. Given the examples she'd had in her life, she had no confidence in her ability to parent. It was the other reason she'd never given serious thought to having kids of her own. But now the one man who had captured her heart like no other came as a package deal. Take one, take them both.

She knew some people would say she was foolish for looking into the future like that, but for Violet, she wouldn't consider a relationship unless the ultimate goal was marriage. She wasn't one for dating around, so she had to think in terms of not just becoming a wife, but a mother too. Even at this budding stage of their relationship, she had to think of those things. Because if she just couldn't see herself as a mother to Dean's child, there was no reason to continue the relationship.

৩৯৩

"Well, the car is here, but I just got home. Let me go see if she's in her room," Jessa said when Dean called. "You might try her cell. Do you have the number?"

"I've already tried that. No answer."

"Well, she's not in her room. Must be out for a hike or something. Although it's not like her to not answer her cell."

Dean had called Jessa on the office phone, so while he was talking to her, he picked up his cell and tried to call Violet again.

"Hang on," Jessa said. "I hear a phone ringing in the kitchen. Huh. That's weird."

"What?" Dean asked as he tapped the screen to end the call.

"That was her phone ringing. Your number was on the screen."

"Her cell phone is there? But she's not?" Dean tried to keep the concern out of his voice, but clearly failed when there was silence on the other end of the line.

"What's going on, Dean?" Jessa demanded, her tone anxious. "What's happened to Violet?"

Dean debated for a split second over what to do. "I'm afraid I made a mistake with your sister."

"I'm more than a little confused here," Jessa said, her

voice still tense. "What is going on?"

Dean rubbed his forehead. "Violet and I have been spending time together, to see if maybe a relationship might work for us."

"You and Violet? Well, I sort of saw that one coming, but she never said anything, so I figured you hadn't made a move."

"Yes, she was quite determined to keep people from knowing until she was more sure about how she felt."

"She's always been a good one for keeping her feelings to herself," Jessa said. "So what happened?"

"I didn't tell her about Addy. She found out from someone else."

"Oh boy. Yeah, you did make a mistake. Violet doesn't trust easily." Jessa's sigh was audible. "Why didn't you tell her?"

"A few different reasons. None of which seem to be significant now," Dean admitted. Right then, all that was important was trying to repair the damage he'd done by keeping his secret.

"I always credited you with more smarts than that," Jessa commented bluntly. "You took quite a risk in thinking that no one would mention Addy to her. In fact, I probably would have told her myself if I'd had a clue she was that interested in you. But since she didn't discuss you with me, I never had the opportunity."

"Let's just say I was leading with my heart, not my head this time around. Obviously I'd do it differently if I had the chance."

"Well, I'll let her know you're trying to reach her when she gets home. No guarantees on what she does then though."

Jessa certainly wasn't one to crusade for love, Dean thought dismally. Yes, he'd messed up, but he had hoped that maybe she'd be willing to help him get her sister to give him another chance. Or at least listen to what he had to say.

"Okay, thanks." Dean hung up the phone with a sigh. He supposed this was what happened when someone spent more time focused on a career than relationships. The only relationship he'd spent any amount of time on lately had been the one as father to Addy. He really missed his sister at times like this. No doubt she would have had some wisdom for him. Of course, the whole situation wouldn't have even occurred had his sister been alive.

He was almost forty and still bumbling his way through a relationship. It's no wonder the only serious one in his past had ended in divorce. No doubt his ex would have loved to give him some pointers on all the things he'd done wrong...after she told him where to go.

But his job didn't allow him to wallow in his misery too long. Phone calls came in. People stopped by. Deputies reported to him. Life went on.

ဆာ

As the sun began its downward trek toward the tops of the trees, Violet reached into her pocket for her phone to see the time. Except for the bottle of water and her keys, it was empty. She patted the pockets of her jeans, but they held nothing. Concerned that she'd dropped it on the way, Violet quickly set out along the path she'd taken earlier. She didn't want to be finishing the hike too late, plus she wouldn't be able to see the phone on the ground if it got too dark.

When she stepped from the forest into the back yard, Violet was hoping she'd left it at the house because she hadn't found it. The last thing she wanted was to have to replace her phone.

"Dean called looking for you," Jessa said as Violet walked into the kitchen. She pointed to the counter with the knife she held. "You left your phone."

"Great! I was wondering what I'd done with that." Violet picked it up and pressed a button to light up the screen. Her alerts showed she had a couple of missed calls and some text messages. Not wanting to deal with them in front of Jessa, she slid the phone into her hoodie pocket.

"Everything okay?" Jessa asked as she resumed cutting carrots. "Dean seemed concerned about you."

Violet wasn't fooled by the casual tone. "What did he tell you?"

"Just that he'd made a mistake." Jessa leaned a hip against the counter, knife still in hand. "And that you two had been spending time together."

Violet nodded. "Just getting to know each other a little better."

"Keeping it all close to the chest, huh?"

"I just wanted to be sure. The last thing I wanted was for everyone to know about us and then have it end."

Jessa waved the knife at her. "It's never really a good thing to start off a relationship assuming it will end."

"I guess I just assumed it was too good to last." Violet settled on a stool at the counter. "I mean, seriously, you've met Dean. He's got it all. No doubt he could have his pick of the women in this town."

"If you like his type, I suppose. And from what I've seen, several of the females around town do. The difference is that he's never reciprocated with any of them. You're the first one I know of that he's shown any interest in."

"Then why wasn't he honest with me?" Violet asked.

"He didn't give me reasons, just told me he'd made a mistake in not telling you about Addy right away."

Violet traced a pattern on the counter. "What's she like?"

"Addy?" Jessa scooped the carrots into the pot on the stove. "She's a cutie. She's like us."

"What do you mean?"

"A little girl without a mother. At least she has a daddy who dotes on her. I know she wants a mommy though."

"How do you know that?"

"My friend, Maura, is her teacher. In December when they wrote their lists for what they wanted for Christmas, a mommy was at the top of Addy's list."

Violet took a deep breath and let it out. "I don't know what to do. It was hard enough to consider settling down in Collingsworth with Dean. Thinking of being a wife was one thing. But a mother too?"

"Isn't it jumping the gun a little to think wife and mother already?" Jessa asked.

"No. I won't seriously date someone I wouldn't consider marrying. And I don't think Dean was wanting us to just casually date. At least we were on the same page about that."

"Are you going to call him back?"

"I don't know. I still don't know what to say." Violet bit her lip. "He hurt me."

Jessa came, slipped an arm around her shoulders and gave her a quick hug. "People that love each other do that sometimes. We've hurt each other. Gran hurt us. We hurt her. But love prevails, and we forgive and move on. Do you love him?"

"Isn't it a little soon to know that for sure?" Violet asked, even though she already knew the answer.

❧ Chapter Seventeen ❧

JESSA shrugged. "I myself don't believe in love at first sight, but only you two can know for sure what you feel for each other. People have gone on to have long happy marriages after knowing each other only a short time."

Love? She was definitely attracted to Dean. She admired a lot of his qualities. They had a lot in common. He seemed to be a man she could love, but did she?

"It's just hard, you know, not having been surrounded by a lot of positive relationships growing up."

"Yes, that's true. Mom couldn't seem to settle on just one man, and Gran seemed content to keep men out of her life. Laurel seems to be only one of us that has it figured out."

Violet glanced at Jessa. "And yet when she was here, I got the feeling that all was not well with her and Matt."

Jessa let out a deep sigh. "Yeah. Me, too. But relationships have their ups and downs. Here's hoping it was just a little blip."

"And it's stuff like that that make me wary of getting involved with Dean. It hurt more than I thought it would when I realized he hadn't been completely honest with me. I can't imagine how much more it would hurt if the relationship ended when we were even more seriously involved."

"There you go again," Jessa pointed out. "Assuming it's going to end when it's barely started. You need to be thinking about it lasting forever, and how you and Dean can make sure that it works out that way. And I'm pretty sure Dean has learned an important lesson and won't be repeating this mistake."

"I need some time. Now that there's a child involved, I need to be even more sure that this is what I want. When I thought it was just going to be me and Dean, I figured we could still do the adventuresome things I liked and travel, but now with a child? I won't just be loosely tied to Collingsworth, I'd be tightly bound. And that was something I swore would never happen."

"I understand, but to be honest, I, for one, hope that you will come home to stay." Jessa stirred the carrots and then put the lid on the pan. "With Gran gone and just me, Lily and Rose...Well, I'd like you closer by."

"I'll take that into consideration," Violet told her. "But I think I'm going to leave town for a few days."

Jessa's brow furrowed. "Don't you think you should work things out with Dean first?"

"No, I need to figure out my own feelings about this. It's not just me and Dean anymore. It's me, Dean and Addy. If I don't feel at peace about that, then I can't have me and Dean either."

"Where are you going to go?"

"I need to go to Colorado to get some pictures for an article I'm doing, so I think I'll head there and then fly on out to Seattle for Lucy's wedding. Hopefully when I get back, I'll have a better idea of how I feel about this whole mess."

Jessa frowned. "I still don't think it's a good idea to leave without at least hearing Dean out, but your call."

"I'm going to take a quick shower." Violet slid off the

stool. "I'll be back down in a few minutes to help with supper."

Upstairs she read through Dean's messages. They didn't say anything except to ask her to call him. Violet realized she was scared to talk to him before she'd settled in her heart if she wanted the ready-made family he came with. Because, too soon or not, Dean Marconett had captured her heart. In talking with him, she might agree to anything, just to be with him, even if it wasn't the right thing. A little girl wanting a mommy deserved one who was there as much out of love for her as love for her father.

୬ఆ

Dean grabbed his phone when it trilled an alert for a text message. When he saw it was from Violet, relief flooded him. At least she was okay. He would have preferred a phone call, but he'd take just about any communication with her right now.

I need some time. I know I said that already, but given what's happened, I need it again.

Disappointment replaced relief. He just wanted to talk to her. To try and explain why he'd done what he'd done. He didn't want to lose her.

Before he could reply, another message appeared from her.

Finding out about Addy put everything in a different light. I need to be sure, for all our sakes. I hope you understand.

And then another one popped up.

I'm going away for a week or so. We can talk when I get back. Take care of yourself.

Dean slumped back in his chair. She wasn't even going to give him the chance to plead his case. He'd tried so hard to control this situation, but now he was left in a position where he had absolutely no control. He hated the feeling. Absolutely hated it. But he would as she requested, because the alternative was to give up on the woman who had completely captured his heart in a way no other woman ever had.

Slowly, Dean tapped out his reply. *I understand. I apologize for what I did. Please be safe.* He wanted to say so much more, but a text message wasn't the place for it. And he wasn't sure he had the right to say any of it to her now anyway.

Hearing a knock on his door, Dean laid his phone face down on his desk and looked up. One of his deputies stood there, file in hand. Dean waved him in, resolutely pushing aside all other thoughts and emotions in order to deal with his job.

જીન્લ

Violet stared at the fragrant bunch of flowers she held in her hands. Had she really just caught the bridal bouquet? The significance wasn't lost on her. For the past week she'd been praying that God would give her wisdom and peace about the decisions she had to make. Would He really use a bunch of flowers and an old tradition to make His point? Unlike the crowd of single women around her, she hadn't even been trying to catch it. And yet here she was, clutching it like it was a lifeline.

She glanced up and her gaze met Lucy's. Her friend lifted one eyebrow, and then smiled as if to say, "There's your answer."

Still not convinced, Violet returned to her seat at the table with the rest of the wedding party. Lucy's older sister was there with her two children. A little girl of about five and a baby. She was helping the little girl with a piece of cake while bouncing the baby on her hip.

"Congrats!" she said when she saw Violet with the bouquet. "Got a guy on the horizon?"

"Uh, time will tell. It's kind of up in the air at the moment."

The baby chose that moment to burp with substance. Lucy's sister grimaced and said, "Oh gosh. I need to get this cleaned up! My husband is helping decorate the going away car. Can I impose on you to hold him for a few minutes?"

Violet hesitated, then laid the bouquet on the table and held out her arms. The soft, warm weight of the baby felt foreign to her. The mom dug through her bag and pulled out a large cloth. "Here, I'll cover you with this. It's what I should have had to cover my own dress."

The woman also left her little girl at the table. She looked at Violet with big brown eyes. "His name's Max."

"Max? And what's yours?" Violet asked. She shifted the baby closer. Though she'd cared for both Laurel and Cami when they were babies, as an adult she'd had very minimal contact with little ones. She had distinct memories of trying to put the lid on a bottle to feed the weeping Cami. She had no idea where her mother was. All the five year old knew was that the baby needed to be fed. She'd laid her on the mattress on the floor where they slept while she got the bottle. As best she could, she'd tried to feed the crying baby while Laurel napped. Violet wished that that had been the only memory she'd had like that, but it wasn't. She had far too many of being a child herself trying to care for a toddler and a baby.

"Emma," the girl declared, drawing Violet's attention from the past. She maneuvered another bite of her cake to her mouth, the fork huge in her little hand.

"Emma? That's a pretty name. Mine's Violet."

"Isn't that a color?" Emma asked.

"Yes. But in my case I was named for a flower. My mom loved flowers. My sisters and I all have flower names."

The girl's eyes widened. "Really? That's cool."

Violet gazed down at the baby in her arms. He had brown eyes like his sister and was regarding her seriously. "Hey, little man. How's life treating you?"

He stuck a fist into his mouth and began to suck furiously. As Violet looked at him and then back at his sister, she realized she did have the capability to be a good mother. And not because she had all the answers or experience, but she could love. And she could know a child. That was one thing she always felt created the gap between her and Gran. The older woman had never taken the time to really get to know her, to know what was important to her.

Maybe Dean's Addy would be completely different from her, but she could learn about the little girl. And encourage her. And love her. Violet stroked a finger down the baby's cheek. He turned his head toward it, his mouth open. So innocent. So dependent. At one time the thought of having to be responsible for another human being would have scared her. And having to make decisions based on the needs of someone else would have made her run in the opposite direction. But now...maybe she was ready to step back into that role of caring for others. The role she'd been able to leave behind when her mother had finally dropped her off at Gran's, and other people had taken over the care of the younger girls.

Lucy's sister returned shortly and took the baby back. Violet missed the feel of him in her arms, but was grateful for the short time she'd held him. There had been no clarity or peace to be found in Colorado, even as she did the things she loved. And in all the wedding preparation, she hadn't felt a definitive answer to her overriding question. Could she put aside her past, her desire to be free, in order to be the wife Dean needed and the mother Addy deserved? Within the past fifteen minutes it had all crystallized into certainty for her. She could do it all. If Dean was still willing to take a chance on her, she could do it.

As she waited in the Denver airport for her connection to Minneapolis, Violet got a call from Tom. With all the turmoil of the past week or so, she hadn't really given a lot of thought to the search. Hoping he had good news, Violet answered the call.

"Sorry I didn't get back to you sooner," Tom said once they'd gotten past the pleasantries.

"That's not a problem," Violet assured him. "Have you been able to find anything else?"

"Unfortunately nothing definitive about your mother." He cleared his throat. "However, I've come across another interesting situation that may or may not tie in with your mom."

"What's that?" Violet tucked her feet under her on the vinyl chair she sat on as she waited for her next flight.

"In talking to the people who last remember seeing your mom around the time Lily was born, I keep hearing about a guy she was with."

"Yes, I seem to remember her coming home with a man. I think I put that in my notes for you."

"You did, so when I had a hard time coming up with info on your mom, I decided to revisit these people and ask if they remembered anything about the guy."

"I think his name was Scott, but don't know his last name. I've always wondered if he was Lily's father, but had no way to confirm that. Mom never listed fathers on the birth certificates which makes me think that usually by the time we were born, our dads had long since disappeared."

"Yeah, from what I hear, the timing of his appearance wouldn't fit with him being Lily's father. It sounded like it was a newer relationship."

"Do you think he would know more about Mom?"

"That's what I had hoped. I was able to get a name. Scott Lewis. But no one remembers seeing him after he and your mom left for Collingsworth. It's like they both disappeared off the face of the earth after that visit."

"That's weird. I remember Mom coming to say goodbye to us girls. She said she'd try and come back to visit and to remember that she loved us. So I don't think she was planning to disappear for good."

"Well, I did a little more digging and actually found a missing person's report on Scott. It was filed by his family a couple of months after his visit to Collingsworth."

"Really? Were you able to talk to them?"

"Yes, I made contact with his older brother. He said they

still hadn't heard anything from Scott. Their last communication with him was when he called to say that his fortunes had turned, and he was finally going to be able to afford the good things in life."

Violet pressed a hand to her stomach and swallowed hard. "Do you think he hooked up with my mom for the money?"

"Anything's possible. Is there any chance your grandmother would have given your mom a lump sum of money to go away and stay away?"

She bit the inside of her cheek and thought back. All she remembered of that time was being so excited to see her mom again and then how disappointed she was when she realized that Elizabeth was leaving again. Scott had seemed nice enough from a twelve year old's perspective, but she knew Gran hadn't been happy with his presence in the manor.

"She might have. Or maybe she gave it to Scott to make him leave my mom alone? I could actually imagine that scenario more than her giving money to Mama." Violet stared out the large glass windows, watching as a plane taxied up to the terminal.

"I'm just playing with a few different scenarios to see if one might give me an idea for a new direction to go in. Any chance your family lawyer might cough up some information that could help?"

"I tried to call him after we spoke last time, but he was out of the office on a family vacation for a couple of weeks. I think he's supposed to be back on Monday."

"I would suggest shaking that tree to see what might fall out," Tom said. "I'll continue searching to see what I can find on Scott Lewis. His brother gave me a bit more information about him—his birthday, social security number and such—that might help me. Once he realized I might be able to give them answers too, he was more than willing to give me what information he could about Scott and his life at that time."

"If this search can bring resolution for two families, all

the better," Violet said. She watched as a woman stepped behind the counter of the gate where she would be getting on the plane. "I'm going to have to let you go, Tom. I'm actually sitting in the Denver airport getting ready to board a flight back to Minneapolis. I'll give you a call on Monday after I talk with the lawyer."

"Just one more thing," Tom said, his tone urgent. "A few of the people I talked to remember your mom being pregnant at a time that doesn't match any of your ages."

"What? Do you think she had a miscarriage?"

"I'm not sure. I'm hoping to contact the woman who initially gave me the information to see if she can give me more details. She wasn't able to talk long the last time I called her."

"I can't believe there's a child out there that Mama just abandoned, but she didn't bring anyone home between us and Lily. At least not that I'm aware of."

"Might be something else to ask the lawyer," Tom suggested.

"Okay, I'll do that. I'll let you know what he says, though I'm not holding out much hope that he'll give me any further information."

"Anything is better than nothing. If I happen to find anything between now and then, I'll let you know. Have a safe trip home."

"Thanks." *Have a safe trip home.* Violet smiled at the words. Yes, she really was on her way home.

✌ *Chapter Eighteen* ✎

DEAN followed Addy out of the room where they held junior church. She skipped along, her dark ponytails dancing as she moved. He was glad she was in such high spirits. He, on the other hand, wasn't, and it was taking a lot of effort to pretend he was.

"Dean!" Hearing his name, he laid a hand on Addy's shoulder to stop her from getting too far ahead of him. He turned to see the mom of Addy's best friend hurrying toward him with her daughter in tow.

"Hi, Alice," he said as the woman and young girl neared.

Addy immediately went to her friend, and they started chatting and giggling.

"Just wondering if it would be okay if Addy came over this afternoon? Rod decided to take the boys to the shooting range, so I thought maybe I'd do some girly stuff with Jade. She wanted to know if Addy could join us."

Dean kept a smile on his face even as a shaft of pain pierced his heart. How he wished he had been able to give Addy the mommy she wanted so badly to do things like this with her. He knew Alice often included Addy in the things she and Jade did because of that. "Sure, I know she'd love that. Do you want me to bring her by after we've eaten?"

"Actually, why don't the two of you join us for lunch? I've made plenty," Alice assured him.

"That sounds good to me. Miss Sylvia is away this weekend, so we were going to just wing it for lunch. I'm pretty sure whatever you're serving will be way better than that."

"Great!" Alice gave him a big smile. "Rod and the boys are out in the car already, so just come over when you're done here."

Addy wasn't pleased to have to say goodbye to Jade, but she brightened considerably when told she would be spending the afternoon with her best friend.

"Slow down, sweetie," Dean said when Addy tried to pull him to the exit. "I want to check our mailbox, okay?"

Addy's lip poked out briefly, but then she settled into step beside him, holding his hand. "Can I check it, Daddy?" Dean nodded and watched while she looked for their familiar last name. "This one?"

"Yep, that's it."

She pulled out a couple of the papers and handed them to him. "Can we go now?"

Dean smiled down at her. "Yes, we can go now."

As they walked toward the exit, Dean spotted Jessa. She caught his gaze and smiled. He smiled back, though seeing her brought a painful reminder of what he'd let slip through his fingers. Just as his gaze moved from her, he saw her tip her head to the side. He glanced back to see what she wanted. Again she tipped her head, and he looked past her.

Violet.

Though she stood next to her older sister, Violet's attention was fixed on Elsa, so she didn't see the exchange between him and Jessa. His heart pounded painfully in his chest. She looked so good to him. So good. Having not seen or heard from her in almost two weeks, he was like a man in the desert who'd just been handed a glass that contained barely a mouthful of water. All he could do was look. It wasn't enough.

He glanced back at Jessa and gave her a tight smile, then turned away. Eager to get out of the church, Dean scooped Addy up and strode toward the glass doors. He pushed out into the bright sunshine and moved quickly to his car. It took him a couple of tries, but he finally got Addy's buckles done up. As he pulled out of the parking lot, he saw Violet walking down the steps with Jessa and the other two girls. He didn't know if Violet saw or recognized his car, but it didn't matter. She was back in town and hadn't contacted him. That did not bode well for things between them.

She had asked for time, and he had given it to her. He couldn't shake the feeling that he'd basically agreed to the death of whatever had been growing between them. Trying to compose himself before he got to Alice and Rod's, Dean took several deep breaths.

"You need to make sure you're a good girl this afternoon, okay, sweetie?" Dean looked into his rear view mirror and made eye contact with Addy. She nodded so emphatically that it set her pony tails dancing once again.

"I promise, Daddy." Then she smiled, and he felt his heart crack a little more. She looked so much like his sister, the twin he'd been so close to and now missed terribly. He wanted to be able to give her daughter everything, but right now it seemed the thing she wanted most was something he couldn't deliver. He'd had a chance, but had screwed up so badly, he knew it would be a miracle if Violet ever agreed to give him a second chance.

Once at the house, Dean parked on the street and helped Addy out. She raced on ahead of him to the side door that led to the kitchen. Dean took the time to gather himself together. Seeing Violet like that had shaken him more than he wanted to admit. He needed to be able to focus on his visit with Rod and Alice, or they'd surely ask what was wrong. He'd shared his pain with no one, and that wasn't going to be changing today.

The enticing aroma of roast beef greeted him as he stepped into the house, and in spite of his emotional upheaval, his stomach rumbled with hunger.

"Dean! Nice to see you." Alice's husband, Rod, held his hand out to him. About the same age as Dean, Rod was a professor at the college. In addition to Jade, they had two boys who were approaching their teen years, though Dean didn't know their exact ages.

"Good to see you again too." They knew each other from the men's group at the church and had spent time together because of events that both Jade and Addy were part of. This wasn't the first time he'd been invited to their home. They'd had him and Addy over not long after they'd arrived in Collingsworth. The two girls had been just about three then and had become fast friends.

There was plenty of chatter over the meal. The boys were lively and entertaining with their stories. Rod occasionally suggested that they take it down a notch, but Dean actually enjoyed the distraction they provided.

He had just finished his dessert and started his second cup of coffee when he felt the vibration alert on his cell. Given his job, he couldn't ignore his phone even when in church or visiting with friends.

"Excuse me," he said as he pulled the phone from his pocket.

Meet me at the lake?

Those five words set his heart pounding. He looked up at Alice and Rod. "Thank you so much for dinner, but I'm going to have to cut this short. I'm sorry."

"No need to apologize," Rod assured him. "We're just glad you could come. I'm going to be leaving shortly with the boys anyway."

After a few last minute reminders to Addy about being good and arranging a pick-up time with Alice, Dean pulled on his jacket and left the house. It wasn't until he sat behind the wheel of the SUV that he replied to the text. There was so much he wanted to type to her. To plead for a second chance.

But in the end, he settled for just one word.

Yes.

He wouldn't assume anything. Just as this could be her wanting to meet him to tell him she wanted to continue what they'd started, it could be her wanting to let him down in person. Oh, how he prayed it was the former. He plucked his sunglasses from the visor and slid them on before putting the vehicle in gear and heading toward his house. He had no idea if she was already at the lake, but the quickest way he knew to get to their spot was to walk from his house.

Once home, Dean decided to change into something more comfortable than his church clothes. It only took about five minutes to get changed and to set out on the path toward the lake. During the hike there, his emotions were all over the place. He had prayed every day, many times a day, for God to give him the grace to accept whatever she decided. But that didn't stop him from playing out the worst possible scenario. By the time he neared the shore, he figured he was prepared for whatever she might throw at him. But he was so on edge he hoped he could hold it together if she told him the worst.

This emotional upheaval was new to him, and he really hated how weak it made him feel. Tears had pricked at his eyes more than once during his walk. Tears! The last time he'd cried had been at his sister's graveside. And yet he'd found himself so close to tears every time he'd thought of Violet during these past two weeks. If she came to him today with the worst, Dean knew he was going to make sure he never again was as vulnerable to someone as he had been to her. It just hurt too much.

As he stepped from the forest to the rocky area of the beach, he spotted her right away. He paused to drink in the sight of her in a way he hadn't been able to at the church. That had been just a sip; this was like a big gulping swallow. She sat on the large flat rock, staring out at the water. The breeze from the lake lifted strands of her hair, strands that he wanted to touch, to run his fingers through.

He tore his gaze from her and stared down at the ground for a moment. When he looked back up, she had slid off the rock and was watching him. Glad that his sunglasses shielded his eyes, Dean clenched his jaw as he walked toward her. He tried not to focus on how wonderful she looked and how much he'd missed seeing her and talking with her. She wore a light colored jacket over her jeans and floral blouse, and she looked just perfect to him.

"Hi," she said, a small smile lifted the corners of her mouth.

"Hi." Dean hated that his voice sounded so rough, but the tightness of his vocal cords made it nearly impossible to speak at all.

Violet tilted her head to the side. "Thank you for coming."

Dean gave her a short nod, not trusting his voice a second time.

Her brows drew together as she regarded him. Then she stepped closer to him and lifted her hands. Dean inhaled sharply at her nearness and the familiar light musky perfume he'd come to associate with her. Her fingertips touched the edges of his sunglasses, and she pushed them up on his head. Feeling almost naked without the protection of his glasses, Dean let out the breath he'd drawn in and took a step back.

Violet clasped her hands at her waist. "I'm sorry."

Funny. He thought it would have hurt worse. Maybe he'd numbed himself to it by preparing for the worst. In which case, he was glad he'd done it, because the last thing he wanted to do was let her see how much this hurt him. He swallowed hard and, praying his voice wouldn't betray him, said, "I understand."

❧❧

Violet drank in the sight of Dean, noticing a hardness she didn't remember him having before. When she'd pushed his glasses out of the way, she'd seen a flash of emotion so deep, so painful, so hurt that she couldn't do anything but apologize. She had done that to him. In that instant she'd realized just how invested he'd been in their relationship even though it had been so new.

She shook her head at his response. "No. I'm sorry for hurting you, for not realizing just how much was already in your heart before today."

Confusion crossed his face, but he didn't say anything. He just stood there, rock solid, jaw tight as if waiting for the final blow. Violet reached out and slid her hand under his leather jacket to rest on his shirt, his heart. She felt the firm muscle of his chest flex beneath her fingertips as she touched him. Her face warmed, but she didn't move her hand.

Looking up at him she said, "Your heart's already all in, isn't it?"

Another flash of emotion in his eyes, but he said nothing and made no movement.

"I think if I'd realized that sooner, I would have known that you hadn't meant to hurt me by not telling me about Addy."

"No, I didn't mean to." The words came out slowly as if he was having difficulty saying them.

"Why? Can you tell me why you did it then?"

Dean reached up and covered her hand with his where it lay on his chest. Slowly he removed her hand and took a step back. She wondered if maybe he had changed his mind about things between them after going so long without contact. When he lowered his sunglasses back into place, alarm bells started going off. Had she waited too long? Had he decided that she wasn't worth the trouble?

"I didn't want to be attracted to you," he began. "I had heard lots about you from Jessa and Miss Julia. All about how you like to travel and do adventurous things. They doubted you would ever settle down long enough to have a family. So when I met you that day on the road and found myself drawn to you, I fought it at first. But not long, obviously. Then I was worried. Maybe you wouldn't even give me a second look if you knew that I had a child. I wanted you in my life so badly I hid that part hoping you would feel as much for me as I felt for you. I hoped that when I finally told you about Addy, you would accept her because you wanted to be with me. Because you already loved me.

"I knew you were already reluctant to be in a relationship with me because of how it might tie you down. I was afraid that if I told you about Addy too soon that you wouldn't even consider anything with me. I just wanted a chance."

Violet stared at him. She wasn't sure how she felt about his explanation, but then she realized that it really didn't matter. She could see the regret written all over his face. Could hear it in his tone.

"So if you had to do it again, you'd do it differently?" Violet asked.

"Definitely. I would pray harder and trust God to work it out if it was meant to be." Dean rubbed his forehead with his fingers. "Taking it all into my own hands obviously messed it up really bad."

"True," Violet agreed. "But I could have handled it better. I didn't give you much chance to explain."

"I understand. It was a shock." He shoved his hands into the pockets of his jeans.

Unnerved by the sight of herself reflected in his glasses, Violet looked toward the forest. "I've had a lot of time to think. To pray. Honestly, you were right. If I'd known about Addy right from the start, I probably would have resisted any sort of relationship with you. And it wasn't just the issue of settling down. I haven't exactly been surrounded by the best examples of motherhood. I really didn't think I was mother material. And I had actually used your logic as well. We hadn't discussed a family, but I kind of hoped that by the time that discussion came up, you would have been invested enough in us that you would have been okay with never having children."

"So I was right? You don't want children?"

"The thought scared me, so yes, I'd have to say that it wasn't in my plan to have children. But like I said, I've had a lot of time to think these past ten days and I realized a few things. First, my desire to be in a relationship with you is greater than my fear of being a mother or being tied down."

She saw Dean's chin lift and his shoulders straighten. "Second, God helped me to see that no one goes into parenthood knowing everything. No matter how good the examples we have are, in the end, we're going to make mistakes. We're going to stumble around trying to figure out how to do it right, but as long as we have love, patience and understanding, we should be able to make it through those rough patches."

"What are you saying?" Dean asked.

"I'm saying that I want to take a chance with you. I'm going to believe that you see something in me that you think would make a good mommy for your little girl, and trust God to help me fulfill that." Violet swallowed. "If that's what you still want."

"If that's what I still want?" This time Dean shoved his sunglasses out of the way. Gone was the hardness, replaced by joy. "It's all I want."

"You're sure? I'm not used to sharing myself with people. It's going to take some getting used to."

"I love you, Violet. All I want is to know that you love me and, in spite of our rough start, will trust me to never hurt you again. At least not on purpose." He held out his hand toward her. "You don't have to say it back to me. I'm willing to wait until you feel it's right, I just wanted you to know that that's what is in my heart for you."

Violet took his hand and led him a couple of steps to where a log lay on the sand. She stood up on it so they were almost eye to eye. She braced her hands on his shoulders and felt him grip her waist. Looking right into his beautiful blue eyes, she said, "I love you, Dean."

"Are you sure? You don't want to meet Addy first?"

"No, I don't need to meet her. I love you. She's yours, so I love her."

A broad smile broke out across his face. "You really will love her. She's a sweetheart."

"I can't wait to meet her," Violet assured him.

As she stared at him, she saw his expression change when his gaze dropped briefly to her lips. She drew in a quick breath and bit her lip. Immediately his gaze returned to hers. He moved closer to her but then stopped. His face was so close to hers, she could see the flecks of dark blue in his light eyes. And she could feel his breath on her lips.

✑ *Chapter Nineteen* ✑

No," he said as he moved back.

Violet gripped his shoulders, not wanting him to move further away from her. "No?"

"I want you to know everything. It's all moved so fast that we've left out some stuff. Yes, you know about Addy, but you need to know everything."

Violet couldn't very well argue with that. "So tell me."

"Let's go sit," Dean motioned to the rock.

She allowed him to take her hand and lead her to the rock where they sat down side by side.

"First of all, yes, I've been married before and divorced. She thought she knew how to be a cop's wife, and I thought I knew how to be a good husband. After all, my dad had been a cop and had managed to balance his job and family life. The trouble was, I had a lot more ambition than my dad. I didn't want to just be a beat cop like he was. I wanted to climb that ladder and knew it would mean lots of work. She couldn't handle the long hours I was gone. The dangerous assignments I took on. We didn't last a year."

"I'm sure it was difficult," Violet said, not sure what other words would work.

"Yes and no. I wasn't living a Christian life at the time and felt the majority of the problem was her. I felt she just didn't understand me, and how I was working for a better future for us and the kids she hoped we'd have." Dean let out a deep breath. "Having her out of my life made it easier to focus on my goals. And I climbed through the ranks more quickly than most men my age. There was no time for serious relationships, and so, apart from the odd casual dating here and there, I didn't focus on that side of my life much."

"So Addy is not from your marriage?"

"No. About four years ago I had a close call on the job that made me rethink the things I held important in my life. I took on a more supervisory role in an effort to focus on my family. When my sister's husband killed himself, I told her to move in with me until she could get back on her feet. So she did. She and her daughter moved in with me."

"Her daughter?" Violet recalled the story of his sister's violent death. "Addy?"

"Yes, Addy is biologically my niece, but I've adopted her." Dean drew his legs up, resting his forearms on his knees, one hand gripping his other wrist. "When Danielle died, I was devastated. She was my twin. I wanted to take care of Addy, but I didn't know how to do that with my career. I knew I couldn't continue with the long hours, but it was my job, the only one I knew. My parents and I discussed it, and they agreed they would take her to give her a more stable home. But then your grandmother showed up." Dean glanced over at her and smile. "She offered me a deal I couldn't refuse."

"A position here in Collingsworth?"

Dean nodded. "She wouldn't say why she was doing it, just made the offer and let me choose to accept or decline it. She promised me a good job here, a place to stay and someone to help me watch over and raise Addy. It seemed too good to be true, but after another discussion with my parents, I decided to accept it so that I could raise Dani's daughter as my own." He looked over at her, his eyes bright with emotion. "Never in a million years did I imagine that coming here would lead me to...you.

"Addy has lost so much in her life already; I don't want her to lose anyone else. You don't have to meet her right away, if you still need to be sure about us. I know she's going to love you, and I don't want her to do that and then lose you."

"I understand completely." She reached out and rested her hand on his where it gripped his wrist. "I do want a little more time for just us, though. Would that be okay? I'm not looking for reasons for this not to work, I just want you to myself for just a bit longer because it has all moved so fast. A little time to get used to you and me, before it becomes you, me and Addy."

Dean reached his arm out and wrapped it around her waist, drawing her closer to his side. "I agree. I'm not sure I want to share you just yet either."

"Do you have a picture of her?" Violet asked, finally ready to see the little girl she'd soon be letting into her life.

Dean pulled his phone out and after a few swipes of his thumb, handed it to her. Violet stared down at a picture of Dean with a little girl, their faces pressed close together. Both were smiling broadly in the selfie that Dean had obviously taken. It was clear the girl took after her mother, because she looked so much like Dean with dark brown hair and bright blue eyes. Violet touched Addy's cheek with a fingertip and then moved to touch Dean's. "She's beautiful. And she looks like you."

Violet glanced up to find him watching her, his eyes suspiciously damp as he smiled. "Are you saying I'm beautiful?"

"She's the beautiful feminine version of the handsome you," Violet said and reached up to rub the back of her fingers along his chin. She handed the phone back to him. "Take one of us?"

"Gladly," Dean held the phone up and pressed his head

close to hers.

After he took the picture, Violet said, "Please send those both to me."

"I will." Dean slid the phone back into his pocket. He kept his arm around her, and she rested her head on his shoulder.

They talked for a bit longer before Dean pulled out his phone again to check the time. "I'm going to have head back soon. Addy is at a friend's house for the afternoon. I said I'd pick her up around four."

"I understand. Part of me wants to go with you, but that will come in time," Violet said as they slid off the rock.

"Why don't you walk back to my place with me?" Dean suggested. "Then I'll give you a ride to the manor from there on my way to pick up Addy."

Violet didn't hesitate to agree. She didn't want to say goodbye to Dean just yet. He took her hand and together they made their way along the path that led through the forest to near where his house was. As they walked she told him about hiking trips she'd taken around the world.

"Maybe someday we can go back to some of those places," Dean said.

Violet stopped walking, bringing Dean to a halt as well. "Really?"

He turned to face her, brow furrowed. "Did you think I'd expect you to completely give up something you love? I figure that with my vacation each year we can do a week or two with Addy and then a week just the two of us doing some of these things you enjoy as well. My parents would be glad to watch Addy for us."

"Really?" Violet repeated. For some reason she had felt that she had to let that part of her life go when she agreed to consider a future with Dean.

Dean tugged on her hand and drew her close to him. Looking down at her, he said, "Your adventurous spirit is one of the things I love about you. I don't want you to lose that. I would never expect you to give up that side of yourself. It will have to change a bit, just like my life changed when Addy came into it, but there's still room for the things you love to do. You're just going to have a permanent side-kick...if you want."

Tears pricked at Violet's eyes. She bent her forehead to rest it on Dean's chest, gripping his jacket in her hands. *Thank you, God.* Not only had He given her peace about finally putting down roots, He was giving her a man who understood her and still wanted her to do those things she enjoyed.

Dean slipped a hand under her chin and tilted her head back. "I know what you're giving up to be with me here in this town you couldn't wait to get out of ten years ago. Just know that I will do all I can to make it possible for you to continue doing what you love."

"Thank you." Violet blinked rapidly. "Thank you." It seemed to be all she could say.

"You just need to always tell me what you need. I can't read your mind, as much as I'd like to." Dean rubbed his thumb across her cheek. Then Violet felt the roughness of it skim her lower lip. "You've already given me so much. I look at it as my personal duty to make you as happy as possible. I know I'll mess up sometimes, but hopefully nothing will be as spectacularly bad as my first screw up with you."

Violet smiled. "I'm glad to hear you don't expect perfection, because I know I'm going to mess up too."

Dean took her hand once again and led her the last little way to the clearing where they stepped out of the forest. It was about a quarter of a mile walk to his house and once there, they got into his SUV. All too soon he was pulling to a stop in front of the manor.

"I'll give you a call later," Dean said. "That okay?"

Violet nodded. "Have a good evening with Addy."

As she stood on the step watching him drive away, Violet tried not to feel bereft, but she couldn't help wishing she could go with him. And that he had kissed her. She rubbed her fingers on her lips as she turned to go in the house. But maybe it was better to wait. They had time.

Violet rubbed the palms of her hands on her jeans. Dean was due to pick her up in a few minutes. After two more weeks of spending time together and getting to know each other even more, they'd decided it was time to have her and Addy meet. Violet was excited and scared all at once. She felt that this was the point of no return. Dean had already told her that Addy was praying daily for a mommy. She was going to view any woman Dean brought into their lives as a candidate. The last thing Violet wanted to do was break a little girl's heart, so as long as Addy accepted her, Violet was looking at this as the first step to them becoming a family.

Dean had told her so much about the little girl. It was hard to think that she was about the same age Violet had been when Elizabeth had brought her to Collingsworth and left her, Laurel and Cami with Gran. How fortunate that Addy had a parent who loved and doted on her the way Dean did. Maybe life would have been different for them if they'd had that, instead of the strict, distant parental figure Gran had been.

"Heading out?"

Violet turned from the window to see Jessa standing in the doorway of the living room. "Yes. Dean is picking me up, and we're going to have dinner at his place. With Addy."

Jessa smiled. "I hope you have a good time. She's a very sweet little girl. I think you'll love her."

"I know I will. I just hope she'll return the feelings at some point."

Jessa came close and gave her a hug. "Out of us four sisters, I think you are the most lovable. It's no surprise that Dean fell for you out of all the women in this town. And you said you'd been praying about this. Trust God to work it out. I think He brought you and Dean together, and I think you're the mother Addy has been praying for."

"Thanks, sis," Violet said as she hugged Jessa back. "It's just...I love Dean more than I thought possible. I can't imagine a future without him now."

Jessa stepped back and wagged a finger at her. "Uh-uh. No thinking like that. As much as you love Dean, I can see that he loves you. The two of you will make this work. I have every confidence in that."

The sound of a car approaching drew Violet's attention to the window. "He's here."

"Go and have a great evening." Jessa walked with her to the door. "You can tell me all about it when you get home later."

Dean got out of the car as Violet approached. He came around and gave her a hug. "Ready?"

"As ready as I'll ever be," Violet said, smiling up at him.

He opened the door for her and closed it once she was settled in her seat. Back behind the wheel, he glanced at her before steering the car down the driveway. "Don't be nervous."

"That's easy for you to say," Violet replied. "What if she doesn't like me?"

"She already does like you," Dean said.

"What?"

"I didn't want to spring this on her all at once, so for the past couple of days since we decided it was time, I've been talking about you. Telling her a bit about who you are. I even showed her pictures of you."

"Why didn't you tell me?" Violet asked.

"I meant to last night when we were talking, but we got tied up talking about Tom and your mom. But I'm telling you now so you can relax."

Surprisingly, it did help a little, but the nerves still kicked up a notch when Dean turned into his driveway. Violet loved his house and was so pleased that Gran had given it to him. It had a rustic log cabin exterior and was homey and inviting on the inside. It suited him, and if this was where they settled when they officially became a family someday, she couldn't be happier.

Outside the car, Dean held her hand as they walked up the steps to the front door. A warm, spicy tomato aroma mixed with fresh bread greeted them, causing Violet's stomach to rumble.

"Daddy!" Addy darted out of the kitchen and flung herself at Dean. He let go of Violet's hand to pick the little girl up. After giving her a hug, he turned to Violet. "Addy, this is Violet. Violet, this is my daughter, Adelaide."

"Addy," the little girl corrected. Then she smiled at Violet. "You're pretty. Just like Daddy said when he showed me your picture."

Violet returned her smile. "You're very pretty too. Just like the picture your daddy showed me of you."

"Do you want to see my room?" Addy wriggled in Dean's arms, and he set her down.

Violet glanced at Dean. He said, "Go ahead. I'm going to see if Miss Sylvia needs any help."

Before Violet could say anything more, Addy took her by the hand and led her toward the back of the house. As she stepped into the little girl's room, she knew that if this had been the room she'd had at six, she'd have thought she'd died and gone to heaven. Featuring a frilly pink canopy bed, the room oozed little girl. A large doll house stood against one wall and another had a desk and a book case.

Addy took great delight in showing her several of her favorite toys. Violet was glad for all the things Dean had told her about Addy ahead of time so she could interact with some knowledge of what the little girl was talking about.

"Come," Addy said as she grabbed her hand again. She led her down the hall a little further and pushed open another door. "This is Daddy's room."

Violet paused, curious, but not sure it was appropriate to go in. However, her curiosity got the better of her, and she allowed Addy to pull her into the bedroom. One wall had French doors that led to a deck, and floor to ceiling windows were framed by heavy navy blue and burgundy curtains. The view of the forest was something Violet would love to wake to each morning. She glanced around the rest of the room. The bed dominated it. She thought it looked like the log beds made by the Amish, and it had a high mattress covered by a spread that matched the curtains. A television was attached on the wall above a stone fireplace in the corner of the room. On the other wall there was a door that Violet assumed led to the bathroom. She caught a faint whiff of the cologne he wore.

"I see you're getting the full tour."

∾ *Chapter Twenty* ∾

VIOLET spun around to see Dean leaning against the door jam, arms crossed over his chest. One corner of his mouth lifted in a smile. Inadvertently, she glanced at the bed and then back at him. Heat crept up her cheeks as she saw the teasing look in his eyes.

"Well, my ladies," he said as he pushed away from the door. "How about we go eat some supper?"

They gave Addy free rein over the conversation, so she could ask questions or talk about whatever she wanted. Violet loved seeing Dean interact with the little girl. He was a wonderful father for her, and she found herself falling even more in love with him for that. After they had dessert and cleaned up, Addy began to go through the steps to get ready for bed. She brushed her teeth and changed into her pajamas then came out of her room with a book.

"Maybe we'll skip tonight, sweetie," Dean suggested.

Addy scowled. "Why? You said we'd read a chapter every night. And I want to do it with Violet too."

"Okay, but we'll read it in your room tonight."

Another shake of dark curls. Dean sighed. "Okay, off we

go." He held out his hand to Violet. Hand in hand they followed the little girl down the hallway and into Dean's bedroom. He flipped a switch that turned on the lights on the wall above the bed. Addy jumped up and settled herself in the middle of the bed.

"Climb on up," Dean told Violet as he walked to the other side.

A bit tentatively, Violet settled in next to Addy. The little girl smiled up at her. "My favorite time of the day. Except for when I'm with Jade. She's my best friend."

Dean took the book from Addy and opened it to a bookmarked spot. Soon he began to read a familiar story, and Violet relaxed into the pillows, loving the feel of the little body next to hers. She closed her eyes as Dean read about the land of Narnia and its inhabitants. The way he read the story drew her in; his deep voice sending swirls of warmth through her.

If this was a dream, Violet didn't ever want to wake up. The chapter was way too short, in her opinion, and obviously in Addy's as well, since she protested when Dean finished. This time he stood firm. "One chapter, that's all you get."

"Please, Daddy, one more?" Violet heard the pleading in Addy's voice and knew she'd be giving in if it were her choice.

She watched Dean as he stared down at the little girl. "Why? You know we only do one chapter a night."

Addy glanced over her shoulder at Violet and then back to Dean. "Cause I want Violet to stay longer."

Dean looked up, and Violet knew he was going to give in again. She smiled at him. "Just one more chapter?"

"Well, I can't resist both of you." With a shake of his head, he settled back against the pillows and continued on.

Addy giggled and smiled at Violet. It was their shared victory. And if there was any part of Violet's heart that wasn't totally committed to these two already, it was now gone.

Violet stayed through the nighttime prayer and tucking in, and then Dean called Miss Sylvia to see if she'd come stay in the house with Addy while he ran Violet home.

༄ঞ

As he settled behind the wheel of the car, Dean realized that for the first time in weeks he had no stress about this relationship with Violet. Addy and Violet had met and gotten along even better than he'd imagined.

"So?" Dean asked as he pulled the car out onto the highway.

"She's everything you said she'd be. She's wonderful."

Even in the darkness of the car Dean could hear the sincerity in her voice, and it warmed him. "I figured you two would get along. And you're already ganging up on me."

Violet laughed. "How could I resist?"

"I ask myself that every day...several times a day. Maybe you can help me to keep her from turning into a spoiled princess."

It didn't take long to get to the turn off for the manor driveway. Dean turned in, but before he got to the final bend in the driveway and the manor, he pulled to the side of the road, put the car in park and shut off the lights.

"Just wanted us to have a chance to talk for a bit." Dean reached for Violet's hand. "I know you've had a lot on your mind after your talk with Tom yesterday."

Violet sighed, and her fingers tightened on his. "I always knew it was a possibility, but I had hoped it wouldn't be an option that Tom would have to consider. And it didn't help any that Stan couldn't...or wouldn't...give me any more information. It just seemed to be all about bad news this week."

"Unfortunately, I know that Tom wouldn't have mentioned it if he didn't have to."

"It makes sense, particularly once he told me what he had found out about Scott Lewis. I mean, he meets Mama and suddenly starts telling his family he's coming into money? Yeah, that's just too much to be a coincidence." Violet shifted in her seat. In the dim light from the moon, Dean saw her turn toward him. "I just can't fathom that a person would kill someone else for money like that."

"People kill for a lot less, babe," Dean said. As the endearment rolled off his tongue, he realized it was the first time he'd used it for her, but it was going to be only the first of many. "I've seen people kill over a twenty dollar drug deal gone wrong. Life is way too cheap for some people."

"Well, I'm not going to believe she's dead until we find the body." She lifted their entwined hands and pressed the back of his hand to her cheek. "Thank you for your help with this."

"I wish I could do more for you," Dean said.

"I think it's better this way. Given how things have turned out for us, I'm pretty sure you'd be trying to protect me from some of this information. But I need to know. I need Tom to not be afraid to tell me."

"Well, you're right about that. We will just pray that that is not the outcome for this situation." Dean leaned his elbow on the console and tugged Violet's hand. "Come here."

She moved so that her face was close to his. The light scent she wore tantalized his senses, and he knew he'd forever associate it with her. He needed to ask her for the scent's name, because he planned to make sure she never ran out of it.

"Tonight was wonderful for me. Having you meet Addy. Seeing you in my home." *And in my bedroom.* He knew it wasn't appropriate to say, but it had kicked his heartbeat up a notch when he'd walked into his room and seen her there. "It just felt so right. Was it just my imagination?"

"No." She whispered the word, but he heard it loud and clear. "It felt right for me too."

Dean slid his hand along her cheek. His thumb brushed her lips as he lowered his head to hers. He pressed his lips to hers lightly. That first feathery contact sent warmth rippling through his body. He had wanted to kiss her for so long. That day at the beach, he wanted it. Oh, he'd wanted to kiss her, but he'd known it wasn't the right time. But tonight,

tonight...it was just one more thing that felt right.

Her hand reached up to grip his wrist as she pressed her lips more firmly to his. He slid his fingers into the silky strands of her hair to the back of her head. He felt her hand move from his wrist to the back of his neck, each holding the other to them. The console hindered any other contact which was probably just as well.

When the kiss ended, Dean pressed his forehead to hers. "I love you, Violet Collingsworth, and I hope you're prepared to have me in your life for a very long time."

He wished that they could get married right away, but he knew that she had too much going on in her life with her family right then to even suggest that. So he'd wait patiently, knowing it would be well worth it in the end.

"Forever," Violet whispered. "And ever. And home is no longer wherever I hang my hat, but wherever you are, because that's where my heart will be."

❧ The End ❧

OTHER TITLES AVAILABLE BY
Kimberly Rae Jordan
(Christian Romances)

Marrying Kate

Faith, Hope & Love

Waiting for Rachel (*Those Karlsson Boys: 1*)
Worth the Wait (*Those Karlsson Boys: 2*)
The Waiting Heart (*Those Karlsson Boys: 3*)

Home Is Where the Heart Is (*Home to Collingsworth: 1*)
Home Away From Home (*Home to Collingsworth: 2*)
Love Makes a House a Home (*Home to Collingsworth: 3*)
The Long Road Home (*Home to Collingsworth: 4*)
Her Heart, His Home (*Home to Collingsworth: 5*)
Coming Home (*Home to Collingsworth: 6*)

A Little Bit of Love:
A Collection of Christian Romance Short Stories

For more details on the availability of these titles,
please go to

www.KimberlyRaeJordan.com

Contact

Please visit Kimberly Rae Jordan on the web!
Website: www.kimberlyraejordan.com
Facebook: www.facebook.com/AuthorKimberlyRaeJordan
Twitter: twitter.com/Kimberly Jordan